EVE BUNTING

If I Asked You, Would You Stay?

D0005172

A Harper Keypoint Book

Keypoint books are published by
Harper & Row, Publishers, Inc.

If I Asked You, Would You Stay?
Printed in the United States of America.
For information address Harper & Row Junior Books,
10 East 53rd Street, New York, N.Y. 10022.
Published simultaneously in Canada by
Fitzhenry & Whiteside Limited, Toronto.

Library of Congress Cataloging in Publication Data
Bunting, Eve.
    If I asked you, would you stay?

    (A Lippincott page-turner)
    Summary: When Crow, a seventeen-year-old
loner, rescues a troubled young girl
from the ocean, his jealously guarded solitary existence
is threatened by his first awakening to love.
    I. Title.
PZ7.B915271f 1984   [Fic]   82-49052
ISBN 0-397-32065-5
ISBN 0-397-32066-3 (lib. bdg.)

    (A Harper keypoint book)
ISBN 0-694-05601-4

Published in hardcover by J. B. Lippincott, New York
First Harper Keypoint edition, 1987

The wind cut through Crow's wet clothes and his head felt hollow. He glanced down at the back of the pale-blue sweat shirt and the sprawl of dark, water-logged jeans in the bottom of the dinghy. There'd been no sound from the guy now for a long time. Not since that whispered "Help!"

"Don't go and die on me now," Crow muttered. He nudged the guy's foot with his own. "Hold on. Just a couple of minutes more."

Crow kneeled down. He plugged the guy's nose shut, tilted his head and began mouth-to-mouth resuscitation. He tried to remember what he'd learned. Blow, breathe, blow, breathe. Twelve breaths per minute. Wasn't that it? But how did you time a minute?

Each time he stopped, he heard air coming out of the guy's mouth. Blow, breathe. How long had he been doing this? It seemed like forever.

And then he saw a small movement under the blue sweat shirt. Crow stopped and looked. The guy's chest was definitely going up and down. He was breathing alone now. He would be OK. There was something peculiar, though. Crow could read the word BLOOMING-DALE'S printed across the front of the sweat shirt, but he was looking at something else. Under the second Bloomingdale's O and the second Bloomingdale's L were two unmistakable bumps. It wasn't a guy he had rescued after all. It was a girl.

For my friend, Martha Jean Tolles

If I Asked You, Would You Stay?

1

Crow stood at the window of the secret room, looking down. It embarrassed him to call it "the secret room." The words were kid words, and at seventeen he wasn't a kid anymore. Maybe he'd never been one.

The words weren't even right. The secret room was really three rooms: an apartment. Beautiful, remote Sasha's apartment. But "secret room" was what he'd thought when he'd first discovered this place behind its wooden panel. He'd tripped over a loose

3

lace on his Adidas as he was going up the stairs of the old carousel building, and he'd gone crashing to the side. At the time he hadn't known what happened when the wall slid away under his hand. Later he'd found the hidden catch. It was so well hidden that he knew it was a million-to-one chance that had let him find it. Inside, the apartment lay shrouded in dust, muffled by time. He could tell it had lain this way for years and years.

Now the secret room, the secret place, was his. It was the first place of his own he'd ever had. Crow's Nest. His. He stood at the window staring down. He'd never do this during the day, because someone below, on the beach or the pier, might suddenly look up and see him, flitting like a ghost behind one of the dirty windows that circled the top of the big, round carousel building. He'd have to be a ghost. All these old apartments had been abandoned years ago. Seven apartments, there'd been. Wrong, Crow thought. Eight.

It was safe to stand by the window now, with the dark outside and only the light from the sputtering lamps on the pier to shine down on the splintered boards. The beach and the sea beyond were white in the glow of the three-quarter moon. All that moved was a big, black dog rooting in a tumbled garbage

4

can. That . . . and someone swimming way out in the ocean, beyond the breakers.

Crow leaned forward to see better. It was a dumb time to swim, and alone too. But nothing around here surprised Crow. Not the young guy who came each morning to kneel on the sand and bow to the rising sun. Not the old lady with the baton who stood in the empty bandstand every day, conducting an invisible orchestra. So if someone wanted to swim at one o'clock in the morning, in October, when the water was probably ice-cold even in California, well, that was his business. It wasn't Crow's.

He walked into the kitchen, closing the door carefully behind him before he lit the lantern. Then he made himself a cup of instant coffee on the Coleman stove, doused the lantern and carried the coffee back with him to the window.

He'd lost sight of the swimmer now. Then he saw him again, phosphorescence trailing where his arms lifted from the pale surface of the water. Wait a second! Crow leaned closer to the window. The guy wasn't swimming parallel to the beach. He was heading straight for the horizon, or for the dark blur of Catalina Island thirty miles away. What the heck was he doing? Didn't he know he'd have to come back?

Crow shivered and wrapped his hands around the

5

warmth of the coffee mug. He wasn't certain when it came to him that the guy wasn't coming back. That he planned to go on and on till he could swim no more. Then he'd stop. And he'd sink. And he'd be gone forever.

Crow knocked on the window. "Hey you! What do you think you're doing?"

Below, on the pier, the dog's ears pricked, and it lifted its head before it went back to eating.

Crow ran to the door, jerked it open and pounded down the stairs.

The carousel horses stood in their silent ring, frozen at the last beat of the weekend's calliope. Crow shoved open the side door.

Now he was loping down the pier, the sea wind gusting against his face, his Adidases thumping and rattling on the loose boards. The dog chased him for a few steps, nipping at his ankles. He yelled at it. "Get away! Go! Get lost!" A flock of sleeping gulls rose, screaming. He pounded through the flock.

The end of the pier faced the sea's emptiness. What was he going to do anyway, now that he'd come this far? Swim in after the guy and bring him back? No way. He should have stopped at the pay phone and called the Coast Guard. But they'd never have made it in time.

"Hey!" Crow screamed into the wind. "You out there! Come on back!" His only answer was the cry of a gull.

And then he saw him again. Just the head. No arms lifting. Just the small, black head bobbing like a beach ball on the moonlit sea.

Below Crow the dinghy from the bait shop bumped gently against the pier. The dinghy! Sure. He remembered the outboard motor in the stern, and he leaped down the pier steps, falling on the last two, almost going into the water himself.

He threw off the mooring rope, pulled on the starter cord till the outboard jumped to life. Then he pushed away from the dock and stood, crouched in the stern with his hand on the motor to steer, the bow cutting through moonlight on a direct course for the horizon. Geez, it was cold! He'd never felt it so cold. He rubbed the spray from his eyes and yelled, "Where are you? I'm coming!" There was no answer. Only the thump of the motor and the watery hiss of the sea swirling past him. Only the white curl and splash of the ocean and a float of tangled kelp.

He began circling. And suddenly he heard him, a small, weak "Help!" Then he saw him too, saw an arm lift, the head bobbing so close that he could almost lean over and reach it. He cut the motor, kneeled and stretched, found a handful of hair, shifted his grip to the shoulder.

"I've got you. Hold on."

He was pulling now at the heavy, slick, water-logged creature, with the dinghy tipping to the side and sea slopping into the boat. In a second he'd slide into the water himself. Lean back then for balance. Pull! Pull!

He had the guy now, had him all the way in, lying facedown on the bottom boards of the dingy. Crow heard him groan. But there was no time for a closer check. He had to get him to shore.

The motor started again right away. Good little, sweet little motor. Crow pointed the boat's nose at the pier and jerked the engine into full throttle.

The wind cut through his wet clothes and his head felt hollow. He glanced down at the back of the pale-blue sweat shirt and the sprawl of dark, waterlogged jeans in the bottom of the dinghy. There'd been no sound from the guy now for a long time. Not since that whispered "Help!"

"Don't go and die on me now," Crow muttered. He nudged the guy's foot with his own. "Hold on. Just a couple of minutes more."

When he had the dinghy tied at the pier, he ran up the steps and looked around. There was no one. No

8

one to help. No one to call for an ambulance. Even the dog had disappeared.

He raced back down to the boat and hoisted the guy, fireman fashion, over his shoulder. On the pier he eased him onto his back and leaned over him. White face. Eyes closed. Dead-looking, all right.

The wind whistled through the gaps in the loose boards. The flags on Moby Dick's slapped at their ropes, metal lines rattling on metal poles. Dead-looking.

Crow kneeled down. He plugged the guy's nose shut, tilted his head and began mouth-to-mouth resuscitation. He tried to remember what he'd learned, tried to remember Coach Mullen putting them through this at the side of the Franklin High pool.

Blow, breathe, blow, breathe. Twelve breaths per minute. Wasn't that it? But how did you time a minute? Coach Mullen always had a stopwatch.

Blow, breathe, blow, breathe,

Each time he stopped, he heard air coming out of the guy's mouth. Blow, breathe. How long had he been doing this? It seemed like forever.

And then he saw a small movement under the blue sweat shirt. Crow stopped and looked. The guy's chest was definitely going up and down. He was breathing alone now. He would be OK. There was

9

something peculiar, though. Crow could read the word BLOOMINGDALE'S printed across the front of the sweat shirt, but he was looking at something else. Under the second Bloomingdale's O and the second Bloomingdale's L were two unmistakable bumps. It wasn't a guy he had rescued after all. It was a girl.

2

Crow carried the girl up the dark stairs and clicked open the door of the secret room. Inside the apartment he laid her on her back on Sasha's Indian rug and ran to the bathroom for a towel. The light from outside cut across her feet and legs, leaving the rest of her in shadow.

Crow kneeled and began to dry off her face and hair. Then he stopped. Stupid! Stupid! What was the sense in just toweling her head? He had to strip off those clothes and rub her down good, and ease her into his sleeping bag. Then he'd grab a dime and run down and call . . . well, maybe he wouldn't. He'd have to carry her outside again. If he didn't, there'd be medics and cops crawling all over the place, and the secret room would be a secret no longer. Besides, it was too cold for her outside. Way too cold. Never mind that now. First, get her wet things off.

Helplessly, he looked down at her long legs in the sopping jeans. Too bad she was a girl. With a guy he'd have had no trouble.

He pulled at the snap on the waist of her jeans, unzipped them and began tugging.

The girl moaned and flung one arm across her face. Crow stopped. "Hey, miss. Can you help me? If you'd just sort of lift . . ." Hey, miss! How dumb could you get? Miss! All this polite stuff when she was half dead. She hiccuped and turned her head away. Shoot! He was freezing his tail off. He needed to just do this and get it done.

He tugged at the bottoms of the jeans, pulling her legs into the air, half lifting her off the floor. The pants came free. Underneath were blue bikini underpants. Crow decided right off that there was no way he was going to touch those. With her shoulders raised he got one arm out of the Bloomingdale's sweat shirt. "Come on," he muttered. "Don't just lie there. This isn't easy, you know."

Suddenly he was mad at her, making him freeze like this, giving him all this trouble while she just lay there. She'd done this thing to herself. She'd swum too far into that endless ocean—accidentally or on purpose, he didn't know which. Either way, he'd ended up with all the trouble. It was always the same with people like her. People like her had rescuers climbing icy mountains or searching arid deserts. Ridiculous. Dumb people giving sensible people problems.

Her other arm wouldn't come out of the sweat shirt, and he'd managed somehow to get the neckband stuck under her nose.

"Come on, come on," he muttered again.

Suddenly her fist hit him under his ear with such force that he fell backward. "Cut it out," she screamed. "Leave me alone."

She'd pulled her head free now, so the sweat shirt dangled in a wet bunch around her neck. Through the haze of pain Crow saw the terror on her face.

"Geez! I'm only trying to help you . . ."

"*Help* me?" She edged back, like some giant crab. "I know how you were trying to help me!"

"Are you crazy?" Crow stood up, rubbing the side of his head. He wouldn't have been surprised to find it smashed in, like a rotten melon. It was too much. After all he'd done, and now she was accusing him of . . . who knew what? Being some kind of pervert, or something.

"Who do you think fished you out of the ocean?" he yelled. "Who do you think brought you here? I

12

should have left you to drown. You'd think you'd at least say thanks." Shivers ran up and down his legs. "Believe me, I'm not in the mood to rape anybody this minute, if that's what you're thinking. If you want to leave, the door's right there, behind you. Here, I'll open it for you." He stumbled past her and flung the door wide. "Down the steps." He strode back, grabbed her wet jeans off the floor and threw them at her. "And take these!"

She was backed against the wall, in deep shadow.

"Ocean?" It seemed to be the only word she'd heard. She pressed her hands to her face. "The ocean! I remember now."

Crow suddenly felt totally drained. "Do whatever you like," he said. "I'm going to dry off."

He left the outside door open so she could go if she wanted to, and he strode into the bathroom, stripping and flinging his clothes into the chipped yellow tub. His only other towel was dirty and bundled in a corner, but he found it in the half dark and rubbed at his shivering flesh. He'd never be warm again, never. Never.

With the towel wrapped around him, he strode through the living room and into Sasha's bedroom, where he kept his clothes. One glance told him the girl was still slumped against the living-room wall.

13

She was making little, gulping puppy noises. Who cared?

He put on his old, gray sweat suit, his warmest socks and his sleeveless down vest. He was still cold and his head ached. All because of you, sweetheart, he thought. Just so I could bring you here and make out with you while you're puking on Sasha's rug.

When he went back into the living room she was gone. Well, OK and good riddance. The next time he saw someone halfway to the horizon, he'd wave and yell, "Have a good swim."

Something bumped in the bathroom and the girl put her head around the door. "I can't find the light switch." Quavery little voice. More puppy gulps.

"There *is* no light." He edged past her and lit the candle that he kept on the tiled shelf. "There's no water either, so don't try using the john." He went and got his ratty old toweling robe and some white socks and left them by the bathroom door. "Dry clothes outside," he called. "Only if you want them. If you don't, don't bother."

In the kitchen he lit the lantern and stove and heated a can of Big Man soup. Beef and barley.

The girl still hadn't come out of the bathroom by the time the steam was rising from it, so Crow poured half of the soup into a mug for himself and

14

stood drinking it. The heat rushed to the bottom of his stomach, comforting him. After a few minutes he began eyeing what he'd left for her. What was keeping her, anyway? She wouldn't . . . His hand froze above the steaming saucepan. What did he have in the bathroom? Razor blades. A bottle of aspirin.

He banged on the door. "Are you all right?" There was no lock, but she might bash him again if he just burst it open.

There were sounds of retching.

"I'm coming in," Crow said.

She had managed to get the robe and socks on, and she kneeled by the tub, the top half of her body hanging over it. His wet clothes were dumped on the floor. "Sick . . . swallowed a lot of . . . water. Didn't . . ." She paused to retch some more and spoke with her back to him. "Didn't want to use the john."

Crow crouched beside her. "It's OK. I can throw some water in here and wash everything away. The drains still work. Just let it all come up."

She let it all come up.

Crow kneeled beside her and didn't look at what spewed into the bathtub. He tried not to breathe, because it didn't smell so hot either.

After a few minutes she tried to stand, and he helped her.

"I have some soup," he said. "But I guess you'd rather skip that."

She shuddered.

"Look." Crow risked everything and kept an arm around her waist. "I don't know what's going on with you. But is there someone I can call to come get you? Your parents? A friend?"

She shook her head.

"You want me to take you into the emergency room or something? You could be in shock."

"No. I'm . . . I think I feel better. Just tired. If I could sit down."

"Sure." Crow hesitated. He should probably put her into his sleeping bag and try to get her warm. But the sleeping bag was on the floor of the bedroom, at the foot of Sasha's bed. She'd probably panic if he tried to steer her in there. She'd think he had designs on her beautiful body again. He glanced at her sideways and almost laughed. Geez! She wasn't exactly what he'd call irresistible.

He eased her down into Sasha's red-velvet love seat, got the sleeping bag, spread it on the living-room floor and helped her into it. For the first time he noticed the silver necklace that she wore. It was wide and studded with some kind of pale beads that shone against the whiteness of her

16

skin. He zipped the bag tight, closing her in.

"Getting warm?" he asked. It was a dumb question. He could see her shaking through the bag's padding. There was a pink-satin comforter on Sasha's bed. Crow didn't want to take it. It was something personal of hers, and he always stayed away from her intimate things. But this was an emergency.

"Thanks," the girl whispered when he spread it on top and tucked it in around her. "And thanks for coming out there after me."

"Think nothing of it. Sleep. Sorry there's no pillow. I could give you my jacket and you could bunch it up."

She shook her head. "It's OK."

Crow hesitated. "I have to go to work in the morning. I mean, later this morning. So I won't wake you. I get off at four. If you want to stick around till then, it's all right. When I come back, I'll help you get wherever you want to go. Home. Or someplace."

She didn't answer. But after a minute she said in a low voice, "I'll stay till you get back. And I'm sorry that I suspected you. You know, before. It's just that . . . a lot of bad things have happened to me recently. I guess I was expecting more."

Crow stood quietly, wondering if she would say anything else. When he looked down at her a few minutes later, she was asleep.

3

Crow half sat, half lay in the red velvet love seat. He thought he was still awake; but he must have slept, because the girl's touch on his shoulder brought him out of some deep, dark abyss.

She stood in the pool of light that dropped from the pier lamp, the robe clutched around her, the white socks like crumpled bandages below her knees. For a second he couldn't think who she was or what she was doing here.

"I really need to go to the bathroom," she whispered, "and I don't know where to go. Not if you can't use the john."

Crow shook his head to clear it, then wished he hadn't when the sore place under his ear thumped. "Sure. I should have explained it to you. Here. I'll show you."

He got up on stiff legs and padded to the door. "This is a secret door. The hidden catch is here." The panel swung open and he touched the spring on the outside. "When you want to get in, you push this. The apartment is over the carousel, in the same build-

18

ing. The merry-go-round is only open on weekends in the winter. There's a rest room down there with a toilet and washbasin. I use it. Wait while I get the flashlight."

He led the way down the narrow, closed-in stairs, looking once over his shoulder to ask, "Are you all right? Do you need help?"

"I'm OK," she said.

The flashlight hopped in a white circle in front of them on the dusty wooden steps. At the bottom Crow stopped and pointed. "In there. Take the light. I'll wait for you out here."

The girl stood, staring at the carousel. "I used to go to county fairs when I was little. I remember the merry-go-round, and the music, and all the kids squealing."

Crow grinned. "Not just the kids. I worked the carousel over the summer. Me and a guy called Ethan. That's how come I found . . ." He stopped. They were both good at leaving things unsaid.

She was leaning back, still clutching the robe, looking up at the high, dirty windows where the outside light and moonshine filtered through, looking at the circular gallery that ran around the pointed top of the carousel. "Are there a bunch of apartments up there? This place is huge."

"Yeah, a bunch," Crow said. He'd figured that the only way anyone could guess there were eight instead of seven would be to walk around the outside and count the windows. Even then, they wouldn't know for sure about the one that was hidden. Some of the apartments had two windows to the front, some only one. Two of them had three. "All the others are empty," he said. "The tenants used to use these stairs and the side door into the alley. The building's condemned now. It has been, I guess, for ages. Pretty soon they're going to pull the whole shebang down."

"But your place is great. All that terrific old furniture and stuff. Too bad there's no light or water. How did you get it?"

"It's not mine, Crow said. "I'm just using it." He moved ahead of her and opened the rest-room door. "Here."

"Can I flush?" she asked.

"Feel free."

Crow went across to the horses while he waited for her, running his hand over their sleek paint, stroking the arch of a neck, the sweep of a glossy mane. He loved these horses. Maximilian, with his coat dark as night and his garland of silver flowers. Daphne, soft and gray as sea mist, with dainty hooves and elegant

20

head. Zeus, proud and perfect, thundering his end-less way through time and space.

The girl came out of the bathroom and stood be-side him.

"I remember something," she said.

"I wish you a bird in a sycamore tree,
I wish you a butterfly fluttering free,
I wish you a sparkle of frost on the ground,
I wish you a ride on the merry-go-round.

"Horses of silver, horses of gold,
I wish you a wish that will never grow old. . . ."

Her voice tapered away. "There was more. But I can't . . ."

"I never heard that before," Crow said gruffly. The words hurt him, somehow. There was so much ten-derness in them, so much love. Things he'd never had himself.

When she didn't speak, he turned to look at her and saw the shine of tears on her face. "Someone used to say it to me, years and years ago. I think I'd forgotten it till now. I'd almost forgotten him."

Crow took her arm and held it tightly. Something told him that if he didn't, she'd run outside and right back into that cold, dark ocean.

21

4

The girl slept, her face in shadow. Crow stayed awake. As soon as it got light, he took one of his buckets of water and sluiced down the bath where she'd been sick. Then he found the towel she'd used last night, and the backpack that held his shaving gear and soap, and quietly left by the side stairs.

The air outside was fresh, the ocean asparkle. Already a few fishermen leaned across the railing up by the end of the pier where the swell came in from the open sea, where the dinghy from the bait shop was tied innocently to its mooring. Sam, of Sam's Seafood, was unloading tubs of fresh fish from the back of his stinking old pickup. His knee-high rubber boots sloshed through the stream of water from the hose he kept running in front of his stall. He flashed his gold teeth as Crow jogged past.

"Crow-boy! How's it going?"

Crow waved. He knew all the pier regulars from his summer job on the carousel: Dora, who read palms and tarot cards; Biggie, his store filled with shells and mummified seahorses and starfish: Lucy

22

with her coffee shop and eighteen different kinds of doughnuts. None of them knew where Crow lived, but they knew he jogged here every morning and stopped to take a shower. No one asked why. Pier people minded their own business.

Crow stood on the concrete floor of the open shower and wedged his heel in the drain so the hot water could creep over his ankles. The scalding needles beat against the lump on his head. He felt it cautiously. Geez! What a smack she'd given him! She was a tough little roadrunner, but not all the time. What would she do, now that he'd fished her out of the ocean and she had to go on living?

Warm again in his sweats, he jogged back and up the unused alley that linked the pier to the weed-grown parking lot. Behind the thick rubber plant was the door. Crow unlocked it with Sasha's key and ran up the stairs to the secret room.

The girl stood by the window, staring out.

"No!" Crow said sharply. "Get away from there!"

She jumped back.

"It's not just you," Crow said. "I have to stay away from the window myself. Nobody knows I live up here, you see."

Now she had another of his secrets, another part of him that he hadn't planned on sharing.

23

Her eyes widened. "You mean you're not supposed to be here? The person who lent it to you . . . didn't, really?"

"She doesn't mind. And her name is Sasha," Crow said stiffly. "I told you. The apartments are condemned. The public health people would move me out, and I don't want to be moved. That's all." What he'd said was true. It just wasn't the whole truth.

"That's why I don't have a light in the living room. The bedroom has a black shade, so I can have a lantern in there for reading." Stop jabbering, he told himself. Just shut up. Wasn't there something about he who excuses himself accuses himself? But he still kept on talking. "The kitchen and bathroom don't face the outside, you see. They're against the corridor that runs around the top of the carousel, so I don't have to be so careful, except to make sure that the light doesn't shine out into the living room."

She nodded, as if she understood completely and found it all reasonable.

"There used to be a windowshade in here too, but I took it down. It seemed a pity not to have that million-dollar view." Crikes! Now he was talking about the sea where she'd tried to kill herself. He rushed on. "You can actually stand way back here and still see the ocean."

24

She turned to look and Crow looked at her, relieved that *that* conversation was finished. In the sunlight her hair was a strange color. Not red, not brown, but somewhere in between. Her face was all angles and bones, and so was the rest of her, as much as he could see under the raggedy green robe. She was one of the most nothing-looking girls he'd ever laid eyes on.

"I was just thinking how peaceful it seems this morning," she said. "The sea looks so gentle now. It's hard to believe last night was real."

"Hey!" Crow said. "Forget about that. It's over. You won't try anything that dumb again."

She faced him. He saw that her eyes were the clear, bright green of wet grass, so startling in her pale face that he found himself staring at her. The silver necklace with the blue stones gleamed at her neck.

"I don't think I'll ever go in the ocean again. This morning I thought how cold and dark death is. You know, I was trying to come back. I was so terrified at the end, and I knew I didn't want to die, not for such a stupid reason. But I'd gone too far, you see. It was too late to change my mind. Then I saw your boat. I tried to call."

Crow swallowed. This was maybe the strangest, most intimate conversation he'd ever had in his life.

25

He knew so much about this girl without even knowing her. "You haven't told me your name."

"Valentine."

"Valentine? That's a pretty different sort of name!"

"Yeah. My mother told me my father chose it. He was quite a romantic." The green eyes had brown flecks, like minnows swimming in a clear pool. And there was something else there. Hurt, maybe. Too much knowing? "What's *your* name?"

"Crow."

"Crow? And you think Valentine's funny!" Her laugh made her a different person.

"I didn't say funny. I said pretty. And different. I'm Crow because my initials are CRO. The kids back in school decided that was what they wanted to call me."

She had her head on one side. "Maybe, too, because of the way you look. Black hair. Black eyes."

"And a beak for a nose," Crow finished. "I know. How about some breakfast?"

He fixed instant hot cereal, coffee and wheat bread. They ate at the kitchen table.

Valentine stared around. "You manage OK, don't you? I bet you always manage OK."

Crow frowned. "Not always." He stood. "I have to go. You did decide to stay till I come home, right?"

She made wet rings with the bottom of her cup on the table. "Yes. If it's all right with you."

Crow hesitated. "I'll go with you to the bus, or wherever, when I get back. Do you live in Santa Lucia?"

"No."

"In Cordova then? Somewhere else along the coast?"

"No."

Crow shrugged. Somewhere she'd decided, as he had, that it was better to tell as little as possible. That was OK with him. "Well, I'll take you into town, anyway. You can handle it from there."

He left her still making those crazy rings on the table, and went in the bedroom to dress. Bruce, of Bruce's Sports Shop, insisted that all the guys wear gray Jordache cords and white Izod shirts to work. He gave them a thirty-percent discount from stock. Big deal! The stuff still cost a fortune. The girls were stuck for the Jordache pants too, theirs white, their tops red.

"Sporting with class," Bruce said. "The customers think they'll look the way you look if they buy my big-buck brands. They won't, of course. But we'll never tell."

They had all laughed the way they did at Bruce's

27

weak jokes. Jobs weren't that easy to find in a resort town, off season. Crow had been at the shop for only seven weeks, and he figured he was lucky, even though Bruce paid as little as he could. Lucky, too, that Sasha needed no rent. He was even putting money away, independence money, so he'd never have to live anywhere he didn't want to live, ever again.

Crow stood in Sasha's bedroom, under her photograph on the wall, combing his hair in her mirror. The letter he'd written to Mrs. Simmons lay on the dresser. It had taken him a long time to write it.

"Hello from California," it began.

He had worried for minutes over that beginning. Should it be Dear Mrs. Simmons? Or Dear Aunt Lily? She had asked him and Danny to call her Aunt Lily and Danny did. But then Danny was seven years old. He still didn't know that foster mothers almost always liked to be called Aunt. It was supposed to make you feel that they were real family and cared about you. Danny didn't know that that Aunt business meant nothing. Crow did and thought he'd been pretty smart when he'd come up with "Hello from California."

"I've got a job," he'd written. "And I'm living in a real nice place. Don't worry about me. I know I told you I'd be back at the end of the summer when the carousel closed. But I've found this other thing and I'm happy. I can look out for myself now and you can concentrate on Danny." He'd signed it, "Your friend, Crow. P.S. Tell Danny there's a museum close to here where they have a real, reconstructed dinosaur skeleton."

It had surprised him how nostalgic he'd felt writing the letter, thinking of her opening it in the kitchen of the little wooden house. There'd be snow outside, but it would be warm in the kitchen and there'd be the smell of paint remover. Mrs. Simmons was all the time refinishing old furniture, doing what she called "turning junk into treasure." She'd clean off her hands and she'd call Danny to come hear the letter from Crow.

Danny would leave the table where he'd be sitting, drawing. Danny drew pictures from morning till night. When he'd first come to Mrs. Simmons, he'd drawn nothing but heads, great big heads and each of them with only one eye. The county psychologist, Dr. Bustamente, had told Mrs. Simmons that all the one-eyed heads were Danny himself and that Danny only felt like a half person. That's what the one eye meant. It seemed a farfetched kind of explanation to Crow, but Mrs. Simmons went for it, all the way.

Dr. Bustamente said that Danny needed love. Well, good luck . . . Recently Danny had quit on the one-eyed stuff, and now he drew dinosaurs. Whatever they meant, the dinosaurs had to be better than the cyclops monsters.

Crow's letter to Mrs. Simmons was stamped and sealed. He'd put no return address. He wouldn't have, even if there'd been one to put. Crow slipped the envelope into his back pocket with his wallet and key and smoothed his hair one more time.

He found the girl still sitting in the kitchen, where he'd left her.

"You look nice," she said.

"Thanks. Working duds." Crow took a plastic bag from the cupboard, got their wet clothes and towels and dropped them in. "There's a Laundromat a couple of doors from where I work. I'll get these done. Don't you have any shoes?" She'd need shoes when she left.

"I left my boots on the beach before I went into the ocean. I guess I should have left my clothes too. It would have saved you a lot of bother. But then, I didn't know I'd be coming back."

Crow nodded. It was super weird. They were talking about this the way you'd talk about a movie or a book.

"If you use any water from the other bucket, fix the

plastic cover tightly over the top again. I used to leave the water uncovered until the morning I found the dead rat in it."

"Ugh," Valentine said.

Crow grinned. "This isn't the Hilton, you know. Help yourself to any food you want and stay away from the window. See you right after four."

He was almost at the door when she called after him.

"Sasha's not likely to come while you're gone?"

Crow paused. "No," he said. "Sasha's not likely to come."

5

Stopping on the way to mail the letter and drop off the laundry, Crow took twenty minutes to walk to Main and Olive. Robbie Johnson was just unlocking the door of Bruce's Sports Shop when he got there. At twenty-three, Robbie was the senior guy in Bruce's. Kim Hanilea stood beside Robbie. Off-season, the way it was now, the three of them ran the shop between them.

Kim was beautiful. Even this early in the morning. Her hands were thrust deep in the pockets of the parka she wore over her white pants and red shirt.

"Brr." She shuddered. "Cold."

Crow smiled. Kim was from Waikiki. She was always cold.

Robbie threw the door open and grinned at Crow. "That girl needs a hug, Crow." They got along well together.

"I bet Kim would go out with you, if you asked her," Robbie had told Crow. "I've seen those smoldering looks she gives you."

Crow shrugged. He didn't tell Robbie that Kim had asked him out a couple of times, and that he'd always come up with an excuse.

"You must never have checked that lady out," Robbie said. "Man! She's built! And a couple of years older than you, too! Think what she could teach you."

Crow raised his eyebrows in a leer.

He had checked Kim out plenty. That long, shining hair. That creamy skin. The way she filled the red top and the white pants. He didn't tell Robbie either about the dreams of her he had. How he'd waken at night, sweating and shaking. Wake to the cool, knowing smile in Sasha's eyes. Sometimes he thought Sasha's picture on the wall saw too much and that he should take it down.

"OK, Sasha," he'd told her. "I'm human. I work

next to the girl all day, so I dream about her at night. That's all I plan on doing, though."

Today, working in the stockroom, his hands busy with things that required no thought, Crow's mind drifted from Kim to Valentine. He didn't want her in his and Sasha's apartment. He wasn't going to share it with anyone else. Well, she'd be gone this afternoon. He'd make sure of that.

6

At lunchtime Crow ate in the deli next door, picked up the folded laundry and went back to the shop. One of their sales bins was filled with plastic beach walkers. They were pink with white flowers and hadn't been hot sellers. No need to wonder why. He picked out a pair.

"A buck twenty-nine," Kim said.

He put the money by the cash register.

Kim raised one dark eyebrow. "You can't mean you really want these? They're tacky, Crow. Real tacky."

"I know it," Crow said. "They're tacky but cheap." He dropped them into the bag with the clean laundry and went back into the stockroom. Unpacking boxes, checking sizes, clipping on sales tags, he began again to think about Valentine. Well, face it. He couldn't help thinking about her. It hadn't been exactly your run-of-the-mill night. He wondered what she was doing.

Suddenly he remembered his money. His independence money! He kept it hidden in the toe of one of Sasha's boots at the back of her big, old wardrobe. Geez! How could he have forgotten about it? By the time he got back, Valentine could have vanished and his money with her.

He rushed out to the counter and waited for Robbie to finish with a customer.

"Rob? Any chance I could split now? I have to get home in a hurry."

"Are you sick?"

"No. It's not that. I just need to get back fast."

Rob scratched his head. "Hey, Crow. I don't know what to say. Bruce is coming in and wants all that stuff on the shelves by closing. I was hoping I could let Kim help you, but we're swamped up here. Now if it's really an emergency . . . ?"

Crow slumped against the counter. "It's probably gone by now anyway. What am I rushing for?"

"What's probably gone?"

"Nothing." Stay calm. Suppose she did find the

34

money? What made him so sure she'd take it? Because she was a beach person, a street person, a no-roots person like himself. Broke. Desperate. OK, OK. That meant nothing. *He* wouldn't have stolen anything. She could be honest too.

The afternoon was never ending. Just before four, Kim stuck her head around the door.

"There's a sand-castle competition on the beach tomorrow. Want to come play in the sand with me?"

Crow shook his head impatiently. It amazed him that Kim could make even sand castles sound sexy. "I'm not much good in the sand," he said. "Look. It's almost four and I'm taking off."

"In a hurry, huh?" Kim's dark eyes were watchful. "Date?"

"No date." Crow spoke over his shoulder. "Just something I have to take care of."

He was running then, sprinting along the sidewalk with the bag of laundry bumping and knocking against his legs. Hurrying.

There were lots of people on the pier, browsing in the shops, enjoying the pale winter sunshine. Crow slipped through the alley door and ran up the stairs. The apartment door was not tightly closed. What did that mean?

35

Valentine wasn't in the living room. Crow dropped the bag of laundry and ran to the kitchen. Empty too. But something was different here. He had no time to stop and figure out what. She wasn't in the bathroom either. The bedroom was all that was left. She was there, or she was gone. With his money?

He opened the bedroom door quietly. It smelled of Sasha, as it always did, some vague drift of perfume that he'd decided was sandalwood. The room was dim, cold and lifeless.

He crossed to the wardrobe. Sasha's boots stood neatly on their metal stands. Crow saw the gleam of the lizard ones at the back, and he pulled them out. The left one sprang free from the boot tree when he pressed the spring. He felt deep into the pointed toe. . . . Whew! He sank to the floor and counted the bills. All here. All safe.

There was a sound of tapping. Crow froze, listening. There it was again.

He put the money back and replaced the boot before he padded out of the bedroom and through the living room.

"Crow?" A whisper and another *tap, tap*. "Are you there? It's Valentine. I'm locked out. I know you showed me how to get back in, but I can't find the catch."

Crow opened the door. "I'd rather you didn't leave it open."

"Sorry." She stood outside, a brimming bucket of water at her feet. "I used up half your water and went for more. When I was exploring this morning, I found the hose."

So she'd been exploring.

"It's clever the way you brought the hose up on that flat roof."

Crow saw that she was wearing his sweats with the legs rolled up. Her feet were dirty and wet. "I wasn't the one who was clever," he said. "Ethan has pigeons on that roof. He uses the hose to give them fresh water. I just found I could reach it if I pushed up the window in that other apartment."

"I heard the pigeons outside. Are they cooped up? I hate to think of things cooped up."

"No. They've got little swinging doors in their cages. They can go flying whenever they want."

"I'm glad. But man, you weren't kidding about those other apartments. Abandoned! Just that old beanbag chair in the one with the hose. How come Sasha got to keep all her stuff?"

Crow smelled danger.

"And how come this is the only secret one? You

37

can walk into any of the others, right off the corridor. Why is hers hidden?"

He'd been right to smell danger. "Sasha likes privacy," he said. "So. What did you do with yourself all day?" he asked as he carried the water bucket into the kitchen. It was then that he realized what was different in there. Everything had been scrubbed. The stove shone. The old tiles gleamed. The ledges on the wooden cupboards were free from grime.

"You didn't have to do this."

She shrugged. "I wasn't tired. And it's not much, considering what you did for me. But it was the only way I could think to say thank you."

Crow felt embarrassed. All the time he'd been expecting the worst, thinking of her splitting and taking his stash with her. And this was what she'd been doing.

"Well, thanks." He went for the bag of laundry and set it on the table. "I have your clean things. And here." He pulled out the beach walkers. "Gross, I know. But they'll keep your feet off the pavement. Why don't you go and clean up in the bathroom while I put away my things? Then we can get going." He tried to make it all sound normal, as if she'd just been visiting.

"But I don't have anywhere *to* go. I was hoping,

38

maybe, you'd let me stay here with you. Maybe you could ask Sasha. . . ."

Crow stared at her. "Are you crazy?" His place, and she wanted to move in!

"Just for a couple of days till I get myself together. I'm still . . ."

He interrupted her. "I'm sorry. There's no room."

"I'll sleep on the floor in the living room. I don't need your sleeping bag. You won't even know I'm here."

"I'd know," Crow said. "There's no way you can stay."

"I'm staying." She stood defiantly with her dirty feet apart, facing him. "I have a feeling you have no right to be here yourself. There's something screwy about this whole setup, Sasha and . . ."

"You leave Sasha out of this. I don't want to talk about Sasha."

"OK. I wanted you to say I could stay. I wanted it to be nice, because you've been great to me. I owe you—everything. But two or three days won't kill you. And I need those days. It's self-preservation."

"Huh! You weren't so anxious about self-preservation last night, that's for sure."

The ugly words lay between them, and he knew he'd never have said them except that he was so angry. So he'd been wrong to think she'd taken his money and he'd been ashamed. But this was worse. Now she was trying to take away his private space, something he'd never had before.

Her face was paler than ever. "I'm staying. And I don't think you'll call the cops or turn me out. You'd be scared I'd tell someone you're up here. I'm sorry to do this to you, Crow. Honest."

Crow stared at her. "I'll just bet you are." He made no effort to keep the contempt out of his voice. "I'll just bet you're real sorry."

7

Crow went into the bedroom and slammed the door. He couldn't believe this was happening. There was a horrible, sick coldness inside of him. She'd threatened him. She was moving in. Who was she kidding with this two-or-three-days stuff? What would be different in two or three days?

She knocked at the door. When Crow didn't answer, she knocked again.

"What?" Surly voice. OK. He felt surly.

"Is there somewhere I can take a shower? I'm really dirty."

If that was supposed to remind him that she'd scrubbed his kitchen, it did, and it made him madder than ever. That whole kitchen bit was done to soften him up, that was all.

"There are rest rooms at the end of the pier," he said. He opened the door and walked silently down the stairs ahead of her to let her out.

She stood in front of the carousel building, holding one of his towels, looking first to the left, then to the right along the pier. There was a wariness to her, a tenseness in her legs and body.

"I guess it's OK," she said at last.

Crow watched as she hurried along the pier. She was scared, all right. She was hiding from someone or something. And she thought she'd found just the right place to hide.

He sat on a bench, watching the sea, waiting for her. Suppose he went in, locked the door and left her? But he couldn't. She knew that. One phone call from her and he'd lose everything.

A fishing boat, headed for home, cut through the chop beyond the breakwater, gulls darkening the sky behind it. A big, brown pelican glided on rigid wings

41

parallel to the pier, then folded itself and plummeted into the dark water.

Crow loved it here. No way would he let himself be pushed out by this witch of a girl.

When she came back, he let her in and tramped up the stairs ahead of her.

"I can't believe that rest room," she said, her voice breathless behind him. "That place must have some classy clientele. You should read the junk that's written on the walls."

He could tell she'd decided on her approach. He was supposed to forget what she'd said and done and be friends. No way, he thought. It's not going to be that easy.

"It wasn't all junk though. The stuff on the walls. One said:

'A robin is red, a seagull is white,
    I know a Crow and he's out of sight!'

Do you think that was you, Crow? It had to be. There aren't too many Crows around."

Her voice echoed in the old building, ghostlike, eerie.

"It was some girl who had a crush on you over the summer. Probably she came every day to ride your carousel."

Oh, this little roadrunner was trying, all right! Crow pressed the catch on the door and stood silently aside for her to go in. Instead, she stared around the circular corridor, with its shadows and dim, slanting light. "I was thinking, today. It's like a doughnut, with a hole in the middle for the top of the carousel to go through." Her hand swept along the passageway, brandishing the towel. "I wonder what it was like when all these rooms had people, Crow. I bet it was a neat place to live."

Crow nodded toward the open door. "Are you coming in or have you changed your mind?"

She bit her lip. "I'm coming."

Inside, she stopped again. "You know what? I'd forgotten that I'd need soap for my shower. Lucky for me someone left a sliver. I brought it." She displayed it like an offering on the palm of her hand. "It smells like fresh mint after the rain."

Crow pushed past her into the kitchen, opened a can of beans and another of stew and lit the stove. Did she think he'd soften up because of all this soap and "fresh mint after the rain" garbage? No way.

He looked blankly around.

Usually this was the time he liked best of all. Day was leaving the sky outside the living-room window, staining the clouds pink and orange, dropping its colors like a benediction. Sasha's Indian rug gleamed, its old richness reviving in the kindness of last light. Usually he would walk around, loving the apartment, feeling himself at peace. Tonight he felt nothing.

He stood in the kitchen, stirring the food, frustrated by his own helplessness.

"Can I do anything?" Valentine asked.

"No." Suppose he didn't give her any food? Could he starve her out? Impossible. When he went to work tomorrow, she could take what she wanted. And if he stayed home, what then? He'd never be able to knowingly keep someone hungry. He banged the pan angrily on the stove.

When the food was hot, he set two bowls and two forks on the table and lit the candle. They ate with the soft yellow light flickering across the table space between them. Neither one said a word.

When she got up to carry her empty bowl from the table, he watched her secretly. She wasn't really that skinny. She'd changed back into her clean clothes, and as she stood with her back to him at the counter, he saw that she filled out the tight jeans in a way that would make most guys look twice. He was mad at himself for even looking once. He glanced away quickly, before she could turn around.

Crow went into the living room and stood by the

window, looking out, listening to the small, splashing sounds from the kitchen where Valentine was washing the dishes. Down the pier the neon lights in the Chart House restaurant flashed red and blue. A gull on the ledge below the window untucked its sleepy head to pick at its feathers, then slept again.

He heard Valentine come into the room behind him.

"All finished," she said brightly.

"I think I'm going to sack out now," Crow said. "I'm tired. I didn't get much sleep last night."

"I know. Do you go to work tomorrow?"

He debated not answering her. Why should he pretend to be polite? "It's Saturday," he said at last. "I don't go until ten." Then he looked at the sleeping bag and the pink folded comforter on the floor. He knew if he took the bag, she'd have a miserable night. About three in the morning it got so cold up here you could set out water and make ice. Too bad for her. He took the bag.

"Well, good night." She smiled a timid smile.

Crow slammed the bedroom door.

He read for a while, snug inside his sleeping bag, then put out the lantern.

The old building creaked and moved around him. Crow felt he was on a boat at sea, moving mysteriously with the gentle sweep and pull of the ocean.

Rocked. Comforted. His place, his very own. Thank you, Sasha, darling Sasha, lovely Sasha. And don't worry about her. She won't be here long.

8

Crow's sleep was deep and soundless till someone touched his shoulder.

"What?" he asked fuzzily. "What's the matter? Geez, it's you again! Seems like it's always you, waking me up."

Her hand on his bare shoulder was like ice. She took it away and put her finger to her lips. "Sh! Someone came up the stairs just now."

Her eyes were cat green, and he realized he could see her clearly and that sunlight was streaming in behind her from the living room. It must be morning.

"What time is it?" he asked.

She shook her head. "Listen. I can still hear him. He's walking around up here. Oh, help me! Oh, Crow! It's Marty. Don't let him get me. He must have seen me. He knows I'm here." Her voice was frantic.

"Hey! Hey! Wait a second!" Crow sat up. "What time is it?" he asked again.

"Time? I don't know. Crow, please. Don't let him find me!"

The last time Crow had seen anyone this terrified it had been little Danny, crawling into bed with him, nose dripping, eyes dripping. "I'm lost, Crow. Everybody's gone. Everybody's left."

"Sh, Danny, sh. I'm here. It was only a dream."

It was the same now, the shaking and the terror.

"Sh," he whispered. "I'm here. I've got you." He pulled her head down onto his shoulder. "It's OK. It's not Marty, whoever he is. It must be almost time to open the carousel. That's Ethan, the guy I told you about. The one I worked with on the carousel?" He was stroking her hair, crisp and tangled under his fingers. "He still works here weekends. He comes early, before the carousel opens, to leave fresh food and water for his pigeons. He's English. Did I tell you that? He's real little, and he has a bald head and a beard."

He was saying ordinary things, unimportant things to try to show her how ordinary this all was. "He calls everybody 'ducks.' Even me. 'Crow ducks.' Now that's pretty weird."

He could feel her panting against the warmth of his neck. She was shaking so badly that he held her tighter, sorry for her again, wanting only to take

47

away her fear. "Ethan doesn't know we're in here, behind the secret door. Nobody knows. We're safe."

"The secret door." There he was with the kid stuff again. He rushed on.

"Just wait for a few minutes and you'll hear the music start. You know . . . 'I wish you a ride on the merry-go-round'?"

"Sure," she said shakily and pulled away. She wiped at her nose with her arm. Danny used to do that too. She was standing now. Crow looked up at her.

"Who's Marty?"

Suddenly the roar of the music filled the apartment. Valentine pushed her hands against her ears.

BY THE SEA, BY THE SEA,
BY THE BEAUTIFUL SEA . . .

"The carousel's open for business," Crow shouted.

The music blared around them. A little color came back into Valentine's cheeks. It was the first time Crow could remember being glad of the music.

Then the first ride ended and there was a throbbing silence. Valentine took her hands from her ears. "Wow!" she said. As if on cue, the music exploded afresh, whirling around them, bouncing back from ceilings and walls.

48

Valentine stared at Crow.

He could see the legs of her jeans sticking out from under the green robe and the cuffs of the sweat shirt below the sleeves. Her feet were covered with the wrinkled white socks. She'd worn everything she could find, and she'd probably frozen anyway. Crow felt a pang of guilt. He'd known how it would be. Even if he didn't want her around, he shouldn't have been that mean.

"Take off the robe and the socks," he yelled. "We'll go out to eat. I always do, Saturdays and Sundays. I *have* to."

The minute they opened the door, the quality of the music changed, floating around them, losing itself in the open space above the carousel and along the circular corridor.

Crow took Valentine's hand and motioned for her to crouch down. They kneeled by the low wooden partition that ran around the outside of the passageway and peered over. Crow knew there was little danger of their being seen. No one down below ever bothered to look way up here.

Valentine's grasp tightened in his, and she smiled that smile that took away the angles and corners of her face.

"How wonderful," she said, close to his ear.

It was always wonderful to him, however many times he had kneeled here, looking over.

Below them the carousel turned in a blaze of color. The twinkling lights on the merry-go-round reflected in the mirrors in the center, flashing the brightness back. The shining horses plunged up and down on their golden poles, straining forward, running free. They could see the tops of the riders' heads, see the knees frantically clutching the ponies' sides. Everything was a jangle of sound and joy. The big front doors to the pier lay open, letting the white, bright October sun stream in. Beyond was a wedge of yellow sand and brilliant sea. Wonderful, all right, Crow thought. And I love it.

They watched till the ride ended and the music stopped and the carousel began emptying.

Crow realized he was still holding Valentine's hand. Suddenly it felt awkward in his. They'd both forgotten and both remembered at the same time. He let her hand go, dropping it quickly, levering himself up with a grip on the wooden wall. Hand holding was out. It was all right to be sorry for her, temporarily, but hand holding was definitely out.

9

Crow and Valentine drank hot chocolate and ate fresh crullers in Lucy's Cafe. Crow had chosen a window seat, but Valentine asked if he'd mind moving to a dark corner at the back.

"Do you want to tell me who Marty is?" he asked.

Valentine made rings with her heavy chocolate mug on the yellow table. Making rings seemed to be one of her things. Her head was bent so Crow couldn't see her face.

"Was it because of him that you tried to kill yourself?" The words were out, naked and ugly and bare. Crow waited, letting them hang.

"It was partly because of him I guess. He was the worst humiliation."

Crow snorted. "You tried to kill yourself over a humiliation? Geez, Valentine! I ought to tell you some of the humiliations I've had. What did he do to you anyway? Did he beat up on you? Hurt you?"

She gave a short laugh. "He didn't hurt me physically, no. Marty always was real nice to me." Her hand fumbled with the neck of her sweat shirt and pulled

51

the necklace free to lie gleaming in the dull light. Her fingers tracked the blue stones, moving across them the way a blind person's would move across Braille. "He gave me this. Sent it to me, actually."

"It's pretty," Crow said. "I noticed it before."

Valentine nodded and slid the necklace back inside her shirt. "I'll never take it off. Never. I'll ask to be buried in it."

"You almost were," Crow said sharply. Then he added, "Sorry."

She shrugged, watching him over the rim of her raised cup. "It's true."

Crow leaned across the table. "If you care that much about the guy, Valentine . . . maybe you should do something about it. It could be he didn't mean that humiliation bit. Maybe he's sorry. Maybe he's looking for you."

"I'm sure he is." She shivered. "And you were right. Nobody would try to kill herself over a humiliation. Degradation was the word I wanted. Everything was bad, horrible, sickening. But Marty was total degradation."

Crow raised his eyebrows. What had the guy done to her? "Well, look, I feel some sort of responsibility for you. I saved your life, after all. Do you have a home you can go to?"

"You look!" Crow couldn't believe the way this girl changed. One minute she was soft and vulnerable. The next she was that tough little roadrunner again. Her green eyes narrowed. "You don't have to feel responsible for me. I know you're terrified that I'm going to stick you with me. But I don't say things I don't mean, so you can relax. I'll go. In two days. Somewhere, anywhere. This is Saturday. I'll leave on Monday. By then I'll have thought a few things through." She put her cup down and reached her hand across the table. "You think I want to hang around Marty's territory, anyway? I'll be gone by Monday."

Crow took her hand and shook it, feeling somehow foolish and in the wrong.

"Unless," Valentine said. "Unless you ask me to stay."

Crow released her hand and stood up. "I don't think so."

"No," she said. "I don't think so either." She was looking up at him. "How's your head this morning?"

He touched the place where she'd hit him that first night. "It's better. Are you ready to go? I have to change and get to work. Will you stay on the pier while I'm gone? You can't very well hang around the apartment. The music'll drive you nuts."

"I don't dare stay on the pier. Or the beach either. Is there a movie house or somewhere that's dark?"

"The movie house doesn't open till seven."

She was standing now too, and he saw her knuckles white and shiny where they gripped the back of her chair. She was a mole, a thin, brown mole, afraid of coming out of its hole. That panic of the morning was still there, under the surface. In spite of himself he could feel his sympathy coming back. He looked at her and had an idea.

"The library," he said. "It's open. You can sit in a corner and read, with your face to the wall if you like. It'll only be for a few hours. Saturday's a short day for me at work." He had another idea. "And we'll disguise you so that if Marty does see you by some chance, he'll never recognize you."

They went back to the clamor of the carousel.

Later, when they walked down the pier, Crow was sure nobody would recognize her. Valentine wore her own jeans and the pink beach walkers, but the Bloomingdale's sweat shirt was gone. In its place was a white one with a picture of a Disney bird on the front. OLD CROW. Mrs. Simmons had bought it for Crow when she'd bought Danny his tyrannosaurus T-shirt. A Sea and Surf cap covered Valentine's brown hair, and the top half of her face was almost hidden behind Crow's sunglasses.

She walked stiffly, her back rigid. Once she gasped and grabbed for Crow's arm, then relaxed again. He looked where she looked and saw a guy of about twenty, in shorts and a red shirt, a well-built guy with a shock of blond hair. Not Marty, Crow thought, or she'd be running. But someone who looks like Marty. I'll remember.

"Don't worry so much," he told Valentine. "I bet I could take friend Marty if I had to. I bet I'm meaner than he is."

Valentine smiled. "I bet you could take him, all right. But no, you're not meaner than he is. You're probably one of the meanest-looking guys I've ever seen. But you're not mean underneath."

Crow tried for sarcasm. "Naw, I'm a real butter-ball." She'd see if he was mean or not when he put her out.

Her smile broadened. "You only look mean because of those black crow eyes of yours. And that arrogant nose."

"Arrogant, huh?" It made him uneasy to be analyzed like this.

He left her at the library steps. "Here. You'll have to eat. There's a coffee shop on the corner." She took the three dollars he gave her, folded them and put them in her pocket.

"I hate to freeload. When I get settled, I'm going to send it all back."

"Sure you are," Crow said. "And I'm not being nice. I just don't intend to let you get too weak to leave."

"It's not necessary, you know, to go on and on about my leaving. I'm not likely to forget."

"I'll meet you here around two." He was talking to her back as she walked up the steps and through the heavy library doors. He hoped she heard.

All day long he thought about her; that was one of the problems of having someone butting into your life. They weren't the comfortable, warm, happy thoughts he had about Sasha. These bothered him. He hadn't lied when he'd said he felt responsible for her. And that was worse than bad. A guy had enough to do just looking out for himself.

10

She was on the library steps, waiting, at a few minutes after two. He saw her, and there was something about the way she stood that told him she was ready to jump if a shadow slid in her direction.

"Hi," he said.

The black glasses hid her eyes. "Hi."

"Everything all right?"

"Fine."

They walked together through town, her nervousness making him nervous too. His eyes darted here and there, checking for Marty. Which was dumb, because he wouldn't have known Marty if he stepped in front of them. Wrong, he thought. I have a feeling I'd know Marty.

"Did you eat lunch?" he asked. Geez! Now he was sounding like her mother. Next thing he'd be asking if she took her vitamins.

She nodded and dug in her pocket. "Here's your change." There was a dollar and some coins. He decided she hadn't eaten much and decided too that that was none of his business.

"I don't work tomorrow," he said. "The shop closes on Sundays. But I have a job lined up. And I was thinking. You won't be able to stay in the secret room tomorrow either. If you like, you can help me. It would give you some traveling money."

"You mean, for when I go. On Monday? The day you for sure don't want me to forget?"

"That's right." Crow tried not to be irritated. He didn't need to keep apologizing just because he wanted her to go.

"What's the job?" she asked.

"Scraping the bottom of a boat. The guy who owns it lives aboard. He pulls it out about twice a year. I guess Ethan usually helps him. You know, Ethan of the carousel."

"Ethan ducks?" Valentine asked, and smiled.

"That's right. He can't help Lambert this time, so he asked me. That's the man's name. Lambert. He's some kind of artist. He said if I wanted to bring someone to work with me, it would be OK. It's thirty bucks each."

They crossed the highway and stopped on the grassy verge, looking down on the ocean. The beach was dotted with chairs and people. From here, the pier was a gray ribbon across the rippled blue of the sea. A dragon kite, scarlet and gold, sailed against the clouds, dancing to the drift of carousel music that came to them faintly over the buzz of traffic behind.

"I've never scraped a boat's bottom," Valentine said.

"I haven't either. Lambert will be there."

Valentine nodded.

They walked along the grass by the cliff top, Valentine with her head bent as if admiring the pink plastic thongs.

"You're missing a Newporter probably on the way to Catalina with all its sails up," Crow said. "And there's a water-skier hotdogging the waves."

"Sounds nice," Valentine said. But she kept her head down.

They walked all the way to Departure Point before they turned. Then Crow bought hamburgers and fries and they sat on one of the benches overlooking the beach to eat. The wind that always came up towards the end of the day gusted cold from the sea, lifting the top of the sand, whirling it down the newly empty beach.

"What did you do all day in the library?" So help me, Crow thought. Here I am, playing Mom again. He stared into the distance and chewed on his hamburger.

"I read old newspapers," Valentine said.

There was something in her voice that bothered him.

"It's amazing how far back those papers go," she went on. "They keep them on microfilm, and you just put in the little tape and *whizzz!*"

"*Whizzz* what? What did you read on this incredible machine?"

"About the carousel, and when they put up the building. Who lived in all those apartments. There were lots of movie stars and directors and novelists . . . people like that. It was the 'in' place to live, way back then, close to sixty years ago."

Crow watched the Newporter change tack and head back toward Santa Lucia.

"But I didn't find anything about anyone called Sasha. Anytime. They said no one has lived in any of those apartments for thirty years."

"They don't know everything," Crow said. "I bet they didn't report that I live there now. Alone."

Valentine suddenly sat straight. "What's that? Down there, on the sand?"

Crow stood. "Oh," he said. "It's the sand-castle competition."

"Can we go look?" Valentine was running across the sand, stopping to pull off the beach walkers, and Crow ran after her. He was relieved that she'd stopped talking about Sasha.

She stopped at the first sand mound. "Look," she said. "Isn't that clever? It's a mermaid."

"I know it's a mermaid. That's why she has a tail and seaweed hair." Someone had stuck a piece of driftwood upright in her belly button. Crow pulled it out.

"And here's a whale." Valentine scampered around, admiring, and a small, yellow dog came out of nowhere to scamper with her, trampling on the whale's head, reducing it to a scatter of sand.

"Stop it, dog!"

She bent to ruffle the thick, yellow coat. "Are you lost, fellow?" She kneeled, squinting up at Crow. "I have an aunt, Aunt Midge. Actually, she'd really only a friend of my mother's. She takes in stray dogs. Usually she has twelve or thirteen. She lives in Utah, and when she comes to visit us she has to get a dog-sitter."

"That's better than bringing them with her," Crow said. Then he saw that she was looking at something on the edge of the sea. The dog, bored by her sudden stillness, pulled away from her to sniff at a dead crab.

Valentine stumbled over to a house of sand, square with matchstick windows and a shell roof. A path bordered with sea pebbles led to the door, and there was a little garden to one side with sandy hummocks and a shell wall. She stood very still, hunched inside the Old Crow shirt, her bare feet buried in the wet sand.

"What is it?" Crow asked. "What's the matter?"

She kneeled down. "There should be a chimney," she said dreamily, and she scooped sand, mounding it in her hand and placing it on the shell roof. She pointed. "There's my vegetable garden, over there. But where's the lilac tree? Where's Mother's tree?"

"Here." Crow gave her the piece of driftwood, and she planted it by the side of the door.

"It's all going to wash away in a minute," Crow said softly.

"No." Valentine placed her feet between the tide and the house. A curve of creamy foam washed across her ankles and another wave came, hissing in to flood the bottoms of her jeans, taking a corner of the house back with it when it went.

"You can't stop the sea, Valentine," Crow said.

She stood there, and he knew she was looking at her past and that for her, now, this was her house, the home that she'd left or lost, sometime, somehow. Once someone who'd lived with her here had sung to her about birds in sycamore trees, and butterflies and merry-go-rounds. "I'd almost forgotten him," she'd said. It might have been her father, and there'd been a mother too, and a vegetable garden, and a lilac tree by the door. She'd forgotten nothing.

Crow touched her arm. "Come on, Valentine. There's nothing you can do." Another wave came with a roar, rounding off the roof, taking the chimney, changing the house to a shapeless lump of wet sand.

"I couldn't do anything then, either," Valentine

said. "He came. And there's no home, no mother, no love anymore. No nothing."

They stood with the tide boiling around them, and Crow pulled the piece of driftwood that was the tree, rescuing it just as the ocean took it.

Valentine held it against her face. "I don't smell the lilacs," she said.

11

Crow and Valentine bumped along on the almost empty bus on the way to McMullan's Boatyard. Crow's head jumped with every rattle and lurch. He hadn't slept at all last night, trying to keep warm under Sasha's pink comforter.

The only other bus passenger was an old lady with a large shopping bag and a squashed hat who coughed and hacked and spat into a piece of rag. Crow turned his eyes away. Just what his stomach needed this morning.

He closed his eyes and had dropped into a jerky sleep just as Valentine poked him and said, "The driver says we're here."

Crow stumbled out behind her. The old woman

and the bus both stuttered and wheezed good-bye.

It was early and McMullan's Boatyard was still deserted. Three boats had been pulled up on the sloping concrete, high of the tide line. They stood on wooden scaffolding, and more scaffolding ran around their outsides.

"Which one do you think is Lambert's?" Valentine asked.

Crow huddled deeper in his jacket. "You know as much about it as I do."

Valentine glanced at him sideways. "You had a pretty bad night, didn't you? It was nice of you to give me the sleeping bag. I told you you didn't have to." She'd taken off the dark glasses, and she played with them, folding and unfolding them.

"I know you told me. And you've reminded me ten times this morning of how wonderful I was to do it." He wished she'd just shut up and let him sulk.

"Oh, my," she said lightly. "Such manners."

Just then a man jumped out of a red VW up at the end of the boatyard.

"Is that Lambert?" Valentine asked.

"Yes," Crow said.

Lambert came bouncing toward them. He was a long, thin man of about fifty with a long, lined face. When Ethan had first introduced them, Crow had thought Lambert looked just like Dobby, the gentlest of the carousel horses, except that Dobby was younger and Lambert wasn't wearing a garland of flowers. Lambert did have a gold chain, though, and one small hoop of a gold earring.

He smiled at them. "Sorry I'm late."

"No sweat," Crow said. "This is Valentine. You told me it would be OK to bring someone else."

"Fine. Terrific. The more the merrier." Lambert walked ahead of them to one of the boats, a sailboat. "Here she is." He vaulted over one of the crossbars, reaching up to lay a hand on the boat's side, above the line of scummy algae.

Crow walked around the stern. The sailboat's name was written in fancy black letters. *"Macushla,"* Lambert said. "It's Gaelic. It means 'my dear one.' That's what the guy told me when I bought it from him."

"That's a nice name for a boat," Valentine said.

Lambert smiled. "It's a nice name for anyone. And she'll feel a lot better when we get her clean."

"What do we do?" Crow asked.

"First we scrape her, get all the gunk off. And that's not easy. Then we scrub her down, let her dry, and give her bottom a coat of antifouling paint. Good stuff."

Lambert climbed aboard, agile as a monkey, and called down, "Come on up and take a look before we get started."

Crow went behind Valentine. He'd lent her a pair of his cutoffs and the Old Crow sweat shirt.

Halfway up the scaffolding Valentine kicked off the pink beach walkers. They weren't exactly made for climbing, Crow thought.

Her bare legs were right in front of him, so it was hard not to notice them. Actually, he'd noticed them the minute she'd appeared in the cutoffs. He thought they might be the best-looking legs he'd ever seen in his life. This girl could make a fortune, charging people just to look at them. Maybe they could have used a little sun. White legs didn't have quite the eye appeal of tanned legs. Kim, now, was always brown. But he thought it was nice that nature gave a nothing-looking girl like Valentine such knockout legs. Unthinkingly he put a hand on her jean-covered behind to give her a last boost aboard.

"Cut it out," she said, her voice as cold as the apartment had been in the middle of last night. "I didn't ask for your help." The look she gave him over her shoulder wasn't any warmer.

Crow took his hand away fast. He must be going bananas, touching her like that.

Lambert was waiting for them on the deck. "Mind your heads going below."

He slid across a teak hatch and went down ahead of them into the cabin.

There was no room to stand upright, so they crouched. The small table between the long seats moved up and down and Lambert waved a hand. "Bed. I have two singles, or I can let the table down and make a double all the way across."

Canvasses were stacked in the V space in the bow, and the side shelves had fastened-down boxes, the lids now open to show paints and brushes. Crow saw a folded easel.

Valentine looked around. "Oh, I like it," she whispered. "I wish it were mine. I'd sail away where no one could find me, to coral seas and quiet islands. And I'd anchor and slide the hatch across, and be safe."

Lambert looked at her, his eyes soft, his long horse head tilted to the side. "I've had raves before about the *Macushla* being cute and darling. But no one ever wanted to sail in her where she couldn't be found. No one said safe."

Valentine shrugged.

Lambert fixed them coffee and they drank it topside, sitting on the deck with the sun coming warm on their backs and the thick steam rising around their faces. Crow felt himself beginning to thaw, inside and out. He decided he might just make it. He turned to speak to Valentine and saw that Lambert was studying her, holding up a thumb and squinting along it as though somehow measuring her face.

"Did anyone ever tell you you have perfect bone structure, Valentine?" he asked.

Valentine set her cup on the deck at her feet.

"I've been told. I guess it's supposed to be some sort of comfort when you're not pretty."

Lambert stood and put a hand under her chin, tilting her head up. "What you are is elegant, my dear. Don't you agree, Crow?"

Before Crow could speak, and anyway, what was there to say to such a goofy remark, Valentine jerked her head away. Her face was pale. "Don't," she said. "I don't like to be touched." After a second she added, "Sorry."

"I was only thinking that I'd like to paint you. Nothing more, I assure you. In the first place, you're young enough to be my daughter."

Crow stood. "She's not going to be around to paint. She's leaving tomorrow. And shouldn't we get on with what we came to do? You did say thirty bucks each." He felt mad for some reason. It probably still had to do with the lousy, sleepless night.

Lambert's eyes lingered on Valentine. "Right. Let's get on with it."

He got scrapers from a locker and they climbed down and began.

Lambert hadn't been kidding. It was tough work and smelly, too. Every little limpet and barnacle and fluted shell clung fiercely to its home territory. It hurt Crow to pry them off, though they were already withering and dying on the dry hull. Silly to think they cared. Silly to let it remind him of how many times he'd been pried away from *his* places.

He heard Valentine scraping on the other side. From time to time he heard Lambert talking to her.

"I haven't seen you around. Have you been in Santa Lucia long?"

"Not long."

"Are you and Crow an item?"

Crow rolled his eyes. How dated! And how Hollywood!

He heard the smile in Valentine's voice. "No item."

Later Lambert asked, "Where are you from, originally, Valentine?"

"Oh, parts east," Valentine said.

"New York?"

"That's too far east."

"And you're leaving California and going back there tomorrow, huh?"

"I'm leaving here. But I'm not going back there."

Crow went on scraping. It was funny how he knew every shade of Valentine's voice, how it could change from smart and flip to soft and unsure. He could see her too, in his mind, the way the green eyes would darken with the thoughts moving behind them. It really was strange how clearly he could picture her. Maybe real pretty girls were harder to remember. . . .

Then Lambert's voice came to him, low and intense.

"I don't suppose I could persuade you to move in with me for a few days? I meant it that I'd like to paint you."

Crow stood with his scraper poised, listening to Valentine's silence.

"It would be strictly business." Lambert said. "I'd pay you scale and you'd stay with me on the boat till we got the portrait finished. It's awful pretty out on the mooring. And it's safe," Lambert added gently. "You'd be safe with me. And safe from everyone else."

"I don't think that would work," Valentine said. "But thanks anyway."

Crow was shaken again at his own anger. He began to chip furiously at the barnacles. What was eating him? He wanted her gone, and where she went was none of his business.

When Lambert came pussyfooting around the bow, Crow could hardly stand to look at him.

It took them till noon to get the scraping finished. Lambert went over the hull with sandpaper and hosed it off. Then he shinnied aboard to make sandwiches and pull some Cokes out of the icebox.

Valentine sat on a plank next to Crow. "How's it going, Crow?" She licked at a bleeding knuckle. "This guy doesn't overpay, does he?"

Crow could hardly stand to look at her either.

"Lambert would probably give you more, if you asked him nicely." He moved a little away from her.

"You've got gook on your nose," Valentine said mildly.

Crow glanced at her and away. "*You've* got it all over."

Lambert threw down a bar of soap and a towel and they washed under the hose before they ate. Afterward they spread the red antifouling paint.

By four-thirty they were finished and Lambert gave them each their thirty dollars. He nodded toward his VW. "Want a ride into town?"

"It's OK," Crow said. "We'll take the bus."

Lambert shook Crow's hand, grabbing it before he could object. And why should he object? Lambert hadn't done anything to him.

"I'm on a mooring on Abalone Bay, Valentine, if you change your mind. The *Macushla* will be back in the water tomorrow. Anybody will row you out. I mean, of course, if you're really leaving wherever you are and need somewhere to stay."

Valentine sat to pull on her beach walkers. "Oh, I'm really leaving where I am, all right. But don't expect me on the *Macushla*." There was paint on her cap and on the Old Crow shirt. Her knees were criss-crossed with red paint lines. "Then again," she said, "who knows?"

Crow stuffed the thirty dollars into his pocket. "Ready, Valentine?"

She got her dark glasses from the scaffolding where she'd left them, and she and Crow walked to the bus.

What exactly had she meant by "Who knows?"

When they got back, they fixed dinner—canned chili and crackers, with oranges peeled and sliced for dessert. Valentine had put the piece of forked drift-wood in a bottle, and its branches' shadow flickered

72

in the candlelight. Afterward they washed up and then went together to the showers.

It was cold walking back along the pier. Valentine shivered. "California's funny. It's summer in the daytime and winter at night. Back home it's cold at this time of year, day and night. You know where you are."

"Same where I come from," Crow said. "They're probably having snow right now."

They leaned across the railing looking down into the water where the moon spilled silver. Music and laughter drifted out from the Chart House. Crow started to ask her when she planned to leave tomorrow and stopped. Valentine knew he expected her to go. But no one wanted to have that kind of thing rubbed in.

Back in the apartment they stood in the dim light of the living room. Valentine took her money from her pocket, unfolded one of the ten-dollar bills and gave it to Crow. "For my share of the meals."

"I don't want it. You'll need it." Crow turned away.

She put her arms around his waist from behind and slipped the bill into the pocket of his sweat shirt. "Twenty will be enough," she said. "If you don't take it now, I'll leave it when I go."

73

For a second he felt her close, felt her arms around him, smelled the soap smell of her hair.

Crow stood very still until she stepped back and turned away.

12

This time, when Valentine came into the bedroom, Crow was awake.

He'd given her the sleeping bag again. It was her last night, and he didn't want to think of where she might be sleeping tomorrow at this time. Fully dressed, he huddled with the comforter around him and tried to read by the sputtering white light of the lantern.

His mind kept slipping from his book to today. Valentine. Lambert in his white pants and shirt, as impossibly clean at the end of the day as he'd been at the beginning. *Macushla.* How far could you go in a boat like that? How would it be to have your own little boat, to sail away from everything, the way Valentine had said? Coral seas and quiet islands. How would it be with someone you liked? Crow sat, leaning against the foot of Sasha's bed, looking up at her photograph. Sasha who gave, but who didn't ask for any commitment. Sasha who would never hurt you. She was so beautiful it made his breath catch in his throat. He was still looking at the picture when the door opened.

Valentine stood, blinking in the light, her hair tangled in spikes around her face, the Bloomingdale's shirt with its faded, backward letters touching the bottom of the bikini underpants so she seemed all bulky top and long stork legs.

"Oh," she said. "I didn't see the light under the door. I came quietly, in case you were asleep."

"No." Crow watched her over the top of his book the way he'd watched Sasha. He was suddenly aware that his heart had started a slow, heavy beating.

She hugged her arms around herself. "I couldn't sleep either. I kept thinking about tomorrow, trying to make plans. Then I thought about you in here, cold, and so tired. . . ."

She was shivering, and he shivered too.

"And I thought this is crazy. It *is* your sleeping bag. Why don't we just share it and both be warm? It's OK with me. I know you won't mess with me."

She turned away as if it were all settled and then looked back when he didn't move. "Bring the comforter."

Crow closed the book, set it down, turned off the lamp. He tripped on a corner of the comforter when he stood, and banged his knee against the corner of Sasha's bed. Talk about the too-anxious lover, he thought, feeling his face warm for the first time all night. Except that I'm no lover. He trailed the comforter behind him.

The living room lay in its usual night glow, with shadowed corners and a gold-blue square of window. Valentine was unzipping the sleeping bag.

"Does this open all the way? What I thought we could do is spread the comforter under us and put the bag on top. We can lie far apart and still be warm." She pulled at the zipper. "It's stuck. Can you do it, Crow? My hands are too cold."

He gave her the comforter. "Put this around you."

She was so cool about all this that he felt better. Sure. There was no reason why they couldn't sleep together. It made sense.

He gave a final tug and the zipper pulled free.

"Great!" Valentine lifted the comforter high and let it drift to the rug. Crow spread the sleeping bag on top and they crawled between, one on each side. Valentine was still shivering.

"OK?" Crow sank into the comforter like a bird into a nest . . . a cold, tired Crow bird.

76

Valentine moved, and he sensed her a little closer. He sensed the length of her, the slightest brush of shoulder and hip.

"Cold," she said. "What do you think the temperature is up here at night?"

"About twenty."

"Above or below?"

"Above. There's no insulation, you see. And there are so many gaps for the wind to come through. Of course, it's always cold down here, right on the water, especially at night. The walls are real thin. Just wallboard." He heard himself babbling. All she'd asked was the temperature, and she was getting a rundown on the construction of the building. In a minute he'd be showing her the blueprints. He had a sudden desire to scratch his belly under the sweatshirt and he willed his mind from the itch, concentrating on lying still.

"I was going to take the sleeping bag into the bedroom," Valentine said. "But it didn't seem right for us to be lying where Sasha could see us. I mean, even though all we're doing is trying to keep warm. I thought it might make you uncomfortable. That *is* Sasha in the picture, isn't it?"

Crow nodded. Then he realized she couldn't see him nod and said, "Yes."

"She's beautiful. I don't think I've ever seen anyone that beautiful."

"Yeah. Lambert would probably like to paint her too." He couldn't figure why he had to bring Lambert into this. "Have you made any decisions about tomorrow?" And why had he asked that? Now? Right after mentioning Lambert's name?

He felt her turn so she was facing him. She was so close now, he could smell her skin. He couldn't believe how wide-awake he was. He couldn't believe his heart either. It didn't usually bounce around like this. Maybe he was having an attack.

"I'll go somewhere far from here," Valentine said. "It's no good having to sneak around wearing glasses and stuff. It was bearable for a day or two, to get over the awfulness of everything, what I'd done . . . tried to do. And it was wonderful of you to give me those days. But Marty lives too close. And he likes the pier. He likes places where there's a lot of action. I've been lucky up to now." She lay quietly. "I need to find a job. I need to be self-supporting. Somewhere."

"Have you finished with school?" Crow asked.

"You mean did I graduate?" She gave a short laugh. "No. One more year to go. Ah, well."

"You won't go to Lambert, will you? I mean, it's none of my business but . . ."

She seemed to smile in the dark. "Lambert! No. He's probably nice and kind, all the things he seems to be. But even he scares me." She squinched down under the sleeping bag. "I hate not to trust. I never used to be that way. But maybe I'm coming back to normal. I trust you. That could be a beginning."

They lay still and quiet, warmth filling the spaces between them.

"That sand house?" Crow asked at last. "That was your house, wasn't it? Who did you mean when you said, 'he came'? Marty?"

She didn't answer, and Crow said, "It bugs me when people ask me questions. So don't answer if you don't want. It seems all my life I've had to answer stuff. 'What's your name, little boy? Where did you get those great, big black eyes? How do you like it here? How would you like to have me for your new mommy?' I always hated it. That's one of the things I like best about being alone. There's no one to bug me with a bunch of crazy questions. Just me and the horses, sharing the space."

Valentine got up on her elbow, looking down on him. "But there was Sasha too, wasn't there? When will she be back?" Before he could speak she said, "Great! And you just told me how you feel about questions."

She lay back and Crow let himself untense. Around them in the old building were scurryings and scufflings, little squeaks and shiftings.

"I guess a lot of homeless creatures, big and little, have found shelter here," Valentine said softly.

Now that it was warm under the covers, she seemed very close. When he breathed, he breathed her in. When he turned his head, his mouth touched her hair. He remembered her legs, and at once tried to think about something else. His hand, lying limp at his side, brushed the softness of her sweat shirt where it curved over her hip. He felt his fingers stiffen. He was so intent on not moving them that they cramped. He yawned, pulled his arms from under the covers and stretched. Long shadows moved like tree branches across the ceiling. He turned them into dancing snakes, then crooked his elbow, veed his fingers and made a duck.

Valentine laughed. "Hey! How do you do that?"

"You practice." Crow pulled his arms down and with hands only made a rabbit that hopped from corner to corner, thumped its tail, scratched its ear and hopped back.

"That's terrific!" Valentine sat up, letting cold air seep into their warm nest.

"Lie down and I'll do some more." He did a dog,

80

and a swimming shark and then a dinosaur with a great, long neck.

"That was Danny's favorite. I used to do it on the wall for him."

"Who's Danny?"

"I guess you'd call him my foster brother. We lived in the same house. He had bad dreams a lot, and he'd get into bed with me. I'd do a shadow show for him."

"I bet he misses you. Is he still there? In the foster home, or wherever?"

When Crow didn't answer, Valentine said, "You asked me about the sand house. It did remind me of home. It wasn't that like it, really, except our house was big and square. And it didn't get washed away, just washed away from me. My mother got married again. To a real creep. My own father died when I was five."

"The one who wanted you to be called Valentine? And who wished all those good things for you?"

"Yes. The bird. The merry-go-round."

"But there's still your mother," Crow said.

"There isn't still my mother. She believes what the creep tells her, not what I tell her. She met him last spring at a rodeo in Strawberry Point. His name's Lo Down. It's supposed to be because of the way he sits a horse, but I have my own idea of why he's called that. He . . . he kept trying to hug me and kiss me and stuff. I told him, 'I'm not a little kid, you know.' And he would laugh and say, 'Oh, I can see that!' Anyway, he wasn't kissing me the way you'd kiss any little kid."

Crow lay very still. "So you ran away?"

"Yep. To Marty." He felt her sudden restlessness. "I tell you, I could write a book about running away. First I ran from them, then from Marty, then from everything. And I did it wrong every time." She sighed. "I'd call the book *Valentine's Sure-Fire Tips for Successful Running Away. Dos and Don'ts.* First, have money. Without money you haven't got a chance. Second, know who you're running to, and what's going to happen once you get there. Oh, brother! What's going to happen once you get there!"

Crow lay watching the flickering of light, like sea ripples on the ceiling. In a strange way she could have been talking about him. Except, of course, he wasn't running away. You couldn't call leaving to make it on your own running away, could you? But he had set out without money and without a plan.

"You wouldn't believe what happens to you when you have no money and you're out on the streets with no place to go," Valentine said. Her hands clutched and twitched at the top of the sleeping bag. "Guys kept offering to help me. But some of them . . . well, I guess a few of them were all right. But I got so I couldn't tell anymore. I still can't. Except with you. . . ." Her voice trailed away.

Crow felt so sorry for her, so tender, that he wanted to put his arms around her and hug her the way he'd hugged Danny. He wanted to tell her: "It's all over. It's all over. Crow's here." But she wasn't Danny. It wasn't all over for her. And Crow was here for only a little while.

"Are you warm?" he asked instead.

"Yes. You've been really good to me, Crow. I'm truly grateful. You aren't like a guy at all."

Crow held his breath. It was a good thing she hadn't been able to read his mind since they'd been under the sleeping bag together. But he wasn't sure if he liked having her tell him he wasn't like a guy at all.

"I think you'd better stay for a few more days," he said suddenly. "You still don't have a plan, do you? That's breaking one of the rules of that book you're going to write."

Valentine got up on one elbow again, her face patterned by shadows. "Do you mean it?"

"I mean it. I'll work with you on what you should do."

Valentine lay back. "Thank you, Crow." After a

few minutes she said, "I wonder where the old lady is tonight. The one on the bus? I hope she has somewhere warm to sleep and someone kind to talk to." She sighed. "Good night, dear Crow."

Crow risked brushing his hand against hers. "Good night, Valentine."

13

Morning slanted through the square of window, with gulls calling across the brightening sky and lonely fishermen's feet tramping the pier boards below.

Crow lay awake, listening to Valentine breathing.

He'd slept deeply, waking once to find them lying curled against one another in the middle of the comforter, her back to his stomach, his arm flung across her waist. He'd eased himself quietly away.

Now it was true morning. He tilted his head back to look up and out and saw two of Ethan's pigeons tumbling joyously against the blue of the sky.

It was pleasant waking in the living room. Maybe when Valentine was gone, he'd leave the sleeping bag here. When Valentine was gone . . .

He got up carefully and stood, looking down on

her. There wasn't much to see. She had burrowed herself into the warmth, and only the top of her head showed. That and one bare foot that stuck out of the bottom. He rearranged the bag to cover it.

In the kitchen he heated water for his shave and for coffee. Standing, he ate cereal with canned milk poured over it and scribbled her a note. "—I'll be back at five." He propped it against the lilac and put the ten dollars Valentine had given him next to it.

Then he closed the door gently, making sure the spring caught, and ran down the narrow stairs.

The horses rested, after their weekend's workout, in the dimness below. They never stopped in quite the same place in their circle and Crow walked around, checking where they were, talking to them.

And then he realized that Valentine had come down the stairs behind him and was standing by the rest-room door. She wore his green robe belted around her, and the pink beach walkers.

"I left you a note," he said, feeling like a total idiot. How long had she been standing there, listening to him drool like some big, dumb kid? "I usually visit the horses before I go," he added weakly.

"I don't blame you." She came across and laid a hand on Daphne's mane. "Hi, pretty one. Hi, beauty!"

Crow smiled, relieved. She was going to be a total idiot right along with him. "Do you want to ride her?" he asked. "Get on. I'll start up the carousel."

"You can do that?"

"Sure."

Valentine straddled the horse, leaning across the dainty gray neck.

Crow opened the panel in the center and pushed the green button. The merry-go-round began to turn soundlessly, the horses moving sedately at first, then gathering speed, plunging wildly on their poles.

"No music?" Valentine called.

"Not today. I'd have to plug the calliope in over there. But that would be pretty stupid. It would be one way we'd be discovered for sure."

"Silent riding," Valentine said, her voice carrying back to him over the small creaking and movement of the carousel.

Crow jumped on Maximilian. It was strange riding through the emptiness of the morning, through the quiet, through the little flecks of dust that danced in the slanting sunshine. He'd done it before, here, alone. But it was different, sharing it with Valentine. He could see her halfway round the curve of the speeding carousel, see her and lose her and see her again, and however he urged Maximilian, however he dug with his heels and urged him to go faster, they could never catch up. It was as if Valentine were running away again, but this time from him. He wanted to reach her and hold her and keep her. But of course that wasn't what he wanted. He had what he wanted.

Crow got down from Maximilian and stroked the horse's head. "No more for now, fellow. Maybe tonight. Maybe later." And in some strange way he was talking to the horse and to her and to himself too, for she'd still be here tonight, still with him.

He stopped the carousel and walked through the streaks of sun and shadow to push hard against the big front doors, checking that Ethan had padlocked them tightly on the outside. The locked doors were his safety against the ordinary world.

Coming back, he saw the small pile of envelopes on the wooden counter of Ethan's ticket booth. The letter on top was addressed to him. He knew the writing. It was from Mrs. Simmons and he hesitated, then picked it up and slipped it into his pocket. With any luck Ethan would simply think he'd taken it sometime on Sunday.

Why was Mrs. Simmons writing to him anyway? And why to the carousel? She knew, of course that he'd worked here over the summer. It was probably the only place she could think of to reach him. But why? He knew he didn't want to open the letter and read whatever she wanted him to know.

Valentine was walking around the merry-go-round, the way he had done earlier.

"Will you tell me the horses' names?" she asked. "You do have names for them, don't you?"

Crow nodded. "Sure. But it'll have to wait till tonight. Bruce doesn't like it when the hired help shows up late for work." The letter would have to wait too, but he didn't say anything about that.

"Bye," she called, as he let himself out the side door. "See you tonight."

"See you tonight"! The words stayed with him as he walked along the morning pier, shivering through him. Tonight. Tonight. Tonight.

14

Robbie and Kim were already at the shop when he got there, and so was Joe Hollister, the sales rep for the Wipeout line. Right away he began pumping Crow's hand and smiling his toothy smile. Kim was beaming too, and Crow could see she was bubbling over with excitement.

"What's up?" Crow asked, smiling himself.

"Tell him, Joe. Tell him quick!"

Joe scratched his hair in that boyish way that was another of the Wipeout trademarks.

"Gee whiz, Kim. Give a fellow a chance here. Crow, how would you like to do a magazine layout for me? You and Kim? I can pay you fifty bucks each, or you can take the clothes you'll be wearing."

"Wait a sec." Crow looked from one of them to the other. "I'm not getting this. What layout? What clothes? What's going on?"

"We want you to do a Wipeout ad. It'll run in *Surf's Up* and a couple of other magazines. It'll take an hour of your time tomorrow morning. No more. Confidentially"—*confidentially* was one of Joe's favorite words—"it's a good deal."

Kim squeezed Joe's arm. "And who knows? We could be discovered by one of those big modeling agencies or something, Crow. That kind of thing happens."

"Is it going to be on shop time?" Crow asked. "What does Bruce say?"

"Gee whiz! What do you expect him to say?" Joe showed his perfect teeth. "He's delighted. All this super merchandise can be bought at Bruce's Sports Shop. You can't beat free advertising."

"What do you think, Rob?" Crow asked. "You'll have to be here on your own."

"It's OK by me. I'd go for it if I were you. Fifty bucks beats what Bruce is paying."

"Or the clothes," Joe added quickly.

"But why me?" Crow asked.

Before Joe could answer, Robbie rolled his eyes. "Because you're cute, of course, Crow boy. Just as cute as a button."

Crow grinned. "It sounds good to me. But I think I'll settle for the money over the clothes, if that's all right with you. What time?"

"Nine o'clock. On the beach in front of the merry-go-round. I'll have my photographer there and my Winnebago, so you'll have somewhere to change."

Kim nudged Crow. "I'm wearing one of the new string bikinis."

"You'll start a riot, Kim," Robbie warned.

"Great!" Joe gave each of them one of his cards, though they had stacks of them already in the shop. On the back he wrote: "9 A.M. Photog session. West Beach."

Crow looked at the card. Valentine would be able to watch from the apartment window if she stood well back. Why was he thinking about her again? Why was he getting this shivery feeling? He took a deep breath.

"Hey, Crow! How about pricing those sun visors and hanging them on the rack?" Robbie's voice brought him semi-back to earth.

When Crow left work at five, the fog had come in. He'd seen it hanging in the air at lunchtime when he'd gone out for a sandwich, but now it was solid, blocking out sky and ocean, turning the pier lamps into blurs that shot off splintered prisms of light. If it didn't lift by tomorrow, there'd be no modeling session. Crow wasn't sure anyway how he felt about this modeling stuff. He'd kid about it to Valentine and see what she said.

"See," he'd say, "I have good bones too." And if she asked, "Why you?" he might say, "Because I'm cute as a button." Naw, he wouldn't say that.

The fog had made the world an enchanted place. The carousel building was a deserted castle, its domed top turrets mysteriously hidden by mist. A castle with a princess . . . Crow shook his head. The full moon, not the fog, was supposed to make you crazy. He unlocked the door and went upstairs.

Crow stopped outside the secret door and sniffed. Something smelled wonderful.

Inside, the living room lay in almost total darkness. Fog was a dark gray curtain that hung at the window, shutting out the night.

"Valentine," he called.

He called again as he opened the kitchen door and slid inside, holding in the escaping light.

Valentine stood at the table.

Crow blinked. There were red place mats. She'd cut them from a roll of gift paper that he saw lying by the sink. A big, green fern in a pot stood next to the driftwood lilac tree in the table center, its fronds spilling across the old, cracked wood. Two green candles. A bowl that held four shiny apples. A long loaf of crusty bread.

Crow turned his head slowly. Something simmered on the Coleman stove, something that smelled delicious.

Valentine pointed with the spoon she held. "Beef bourguignon. And you thought I was just another pretty face."

Crow was speechless. He moved to the table and touched a frond of fern. "But where did you get it all?"

Valentine smiled. "That ten dollars? You gave it

back and . . ." She flipped a hand. "I put it to good use."

"No way did you do all this for ten dollars."

"A little more. It's a celebration. A celebration of . . . being alive. And being friends, after getting off to such a rotten start." She touched the fern with tender fingers. "Isn't this beautiful?"

There was a small, pink cardboard box on the counter top. Valentine followed Crow's gaze. "It's a cake. I hope you like chocolate."

"But where did you get everything?" Crow felt suddenly cold as realization came. "You went out, Valentine."

"I know. Don't worry. I put on the glasses and the cap and your big, heavy jacket. I didn't go far. I got everything in that little mall at the end of the pier. Besides, it was foggy." She seemed to sense his stillness. Her eyes were soft. "It's dear of you to worry about me. But I'm safe. There was no harm done. Honest."

"I'm not worrying about you. What I want to know is how you got back in when you went out?"

Valentine stared at him. "I left the doors open, just a bit. Not so anybody could see."

"You left the downstairs door open? And this one too? The secret door?"

93

"Yes. I know you showed me how to open it, but I never can seem to find that catch, it's so well . . ."

"You left the door to Sasha's apartment open?"

"Yes. Yes. I've told you, yes." Valentine wasn't smiling anymore. She carefully put the spoon down on the counter top and smoothed her hands along her jeans.

Crow heard his voice rising and he tried to keep it down. "How could you be so stupid, Valentine? Sasha's place. All her lovely things. Her private life that she guards so carefully, and you left it open for any creep to wander in and find."

"Well, no one did. Besides, I was only gone for a little while. Crow, I'm sorry. I just didn't think."

"You bet you didn't think!"

Stop, he told himself. Stop. But he couldn't stop. "There are always people on the pier, even when it's foggy. Anyone could have seen that downstairs door open."

"I've said I'm sorry. I'm sorry. I'm sorry. Heaven forbid that anyone should see Sasha's sacred things except you. Or look at her sacred photograph except you. You know what I think? I think you're sick. You and Sasha. You're in love with her, with her picture, and she . . ." Valentine shook with anger. Now she was as furious as he was. "I thought for a minute you were worried about me. And that was nice, to have someone worrying and caring about me for a change. But I should have known better! *Nobody* exists for you except Sasha."

"Shut up about Sasha. Just shut up. I knew you'd be nothing but a problem around here."

"Thanks a lot. Well, I guess you were right." She flung the kitchen door open and slammed it behind her. He heard the click as the apartment door opened and the sluff as it closed. He heard her feet pounding down the stairs.

Something was burning. Crow turned out the flame under the beef bourguignon.

15

Crow listened for the sound of the outside door slamming, but he heard nothing. Maybe he'd missed it. Or maybe Valentine had just run furiously downstairs, and she'd come back in a few minutes, expecting him to apologize. Well, he'd never apologize. He'd been right to be mad at her. OK, he'd spoiled her surprise dinner. But she ought to have known that to him nothing was worth the risk of losing the secret place.

He blew out the green candles, went through the living room and clicked the door open. There were the usual rustlings, creakings and squeakings around him. Fog drifted in from outside to lie in the circular corridor, billowing like smoke.

He got the flashlight and shone it down the stairs. No one sat in the darkness but a spider in its web, trapping and holding the light from the yellow beam.

He went quietly down and turned the flashlight on the carousel. The beam moved across the painted backs and gilded manes of the horses. It flashed back at him from the center mirrors, showing only the reflection of his own shadow.

The rest-room door was closed. He knocked. "Valentine?" No answer. He turned the knob and looked into emptiness.

She'd gone out then, into the dark and the fog. He couldn't believe how dumb she was. Where did she think she could go with no coat and practically no money?

Crow made sure he had his key, opened the side door and eased through the alley to the pier.

Every sight and sound was muffled. A foghorn moaned. A seal barked.

Crow walked, shining his light on every green painted seat and into every corner.

A guy and a girl were huddled in the doorway of Dora's Fortune-Telling Salon, their arms wrapped around each other, their bodies welded together. Behind them was the giant hand Dora had painted, its life lines and fate lines spreading like tree roots across the palm. "Get lost, buddy," the guy snarled. Crow turned his light away fast.

He checked the pier from end to end. "Valentine?" he called softly. "Valentine?" Where was she? For a girl who said she knew so much about running away, she'd made a mess of it again, just blundering off like that into the night.

Crow leaned against the door of the shell and rock shop. What now? There was nothing he could think of to do except walk the streets, and that seemed ridiculous. He'd go back, back to the secret room, and think.

He quickened his step, suddenly certain that Valentine would be outside the carousel, leaning over the sea railing or crouched by the alley door. But the railing was empty and the only thing that waited by the door was the rubber tree, its leaves wet and shining with fog.

Inside, he went all the way around the circular

corridor, opening the doors to the old apartments, checking everywhere. On the flat roof the pigeons cooed to one another and to him. He padded everywhere, stepping carefully on the rotted boards. Nothing. No one.

Back in Sasha's apartment again, he lit the lantern in the kitchen and slumped at the table. He wished he could turn time back and be opening the door for the first time, smelling the beef, whatever it was called. If only he hadn't left that stupid ten dollars, she wouldn't have . . . his thoughts came to an abrupt stop. The ten dollars! Lambert! "Anybody'll row you across," Lambert had told her. That's where she'd gone. She'd know the way. She'd ride the bus and get off at McMullan's Boatyard.

Crow stopped only to put out the kitchen lantern and to grab his flashlight again. Better she was with Lambert than out in the streets.

McMullan's Boatyard lay ghostlike and silent. The *Macushla* was gone. Only the scaffolding still stood like some broken dinosaur skeleton. A brontosaurus skeleton, Danny. For the first time all day Crow remembered the letter, still unopened in his pocket. Not now, he thought. One thing at a time.

He walked quickly past the closed marine store

and the lockers and the few parked cars. There was a VW that might have been Lambert's. He paused at the railing, looking across Abalone Bay. Somewhere out there were boats on moorings. He shone his flashlight, but he could see nothing through the hanging thickness of fog. Boats bobbed on slips at the dock. One or two had lights, as though there were people aboard. Crow looked around. There was no one to ask about the *Macushla*.

Crow padded along the swirling dock to one of the lighted sailboats. He leaned over and rapped on the side of the hatch.

"Excuse me," he yelled. "Is there someone aboard?"

The boat nudged at its fender and water lapped gently around the sides. He was just about to knock again when a woman pushed back the hatch and popped her head out like a jack-in-the-box.

"Hi," she said. "What's up?"

"I'm looking for the *Macushla*. Mr. Lambert's boat."

She was smoking a cigarette, and its tip glowed brightly as she pulled on it. "You a friend of Ted's?"

"Yes. I helped him scrape the *Macushla* yesterday."

"Oh. That's right. He did have her out of the

99

water." She coughed. "Well, look. How long are you going to be over there with him?"

"A few minutes is all."

"You can take my dinghy. You know how to handle a dinghy?"

"Sure," Crow said.

"The oars are in it. Be sure to tie her up good when you get back."

"Thanks." She was about to disappear. "I'm semi-lost in this fog," Crow said. "Can you point me toward the *Macushla*?"

She raised an arm. "Straight out. No more than a hundred yards. If you go farther than spittin' distance you've missed her."

"Thanks." Crow stepped into the dinghy and gripped the oars. The last time he'd been in a dinghy it was the one from the bait shop, and he'd been searching for Valentine then too. Why didn't he just let her go?

Fog hung between him and the moored boats. Hulls, fog beaded, rose suddenly and startlingly in front of his bow. A small white duck sailed on the shrouded water, tail held high. Crow wondered if he'd missed the *Macushla*. Could he spit this far? And then he saw it, the letters on the stern appearing for a moment before they were swallowed again in the gray darkness.

He edged the dinghy alongside, laid the dripping oars across the seats and reached up to grab the sailboat's deck. Light glowed from behind the curtained cabin windows. Crow's stomach hurt. What would he say to her if he found her? Worse, what would she say to him?

The dinghy bumped against the boat's side.

"Ahoy on the *Macushla*!" Crow yelled. He tried to hold the dinghy steady.

Lambert's head appeared almost instantly.

"It's Crow. The guy who worked for you yesterday." Crow turned on the flashlight and shone the beam on his own face.

Lambert peered down. "Crow? What's wrong? Come round to the stern."

There was a clatter, and a short hook ladder dropped into the water close to the dinghy. "Tie her up and come aboard."

Lambert reached down to help, and Crow climbed up onto the deck.

"Is Valentine here?" Crow could see down through the open hatchway to the cabin. There was a plate half filled with food on the table, a glass and a bottle of wine. A sketchbook and pencil lay beside the plate. No Valentine.

"She isn't here," Lambert said. "I haven't seen her since you finished scraping. Did something happen to her?"

"She'd decided to stay for a while. Then we had a fight and she just took off." Suddenly he was so tired that he didn't think he could speak another word. He stared helplessly into the fog. Where was he going to look now?

"Come on down and at least have some coffee," Lambert said gently. He urged Crow forward, and when they were in the cabin he put a mug of coffee into his hand. "Drink it. You'll feel better."

Crow felt better after the first sip.

"I'm sorry Valentine didn't come here," Lambert said. "She needed time. If she's running again, she's scared."

"I didn't scare her," Crow said.

"Well then, she's running hurt."

"You sure think you know a lot about her for a guy who only saw her once." Crow knew even as he spoke that he was angry because Lambert was right. Of course he had hurt her. And now he was taking his anger at himself out on Lambert. He forced himself to be half civil. "This is nice," he said, looking around the cabin. "Comfortable."

Lambert smiled. "I like it. It took me a while to know what I wanted and go for it all the way. I was a vice-president in a bank and living alone in the family mansion in Hancock Park. I'd always wanted a boat and I'd always wanted to paint." He spread his hands. "I had to make a commitment, you know. It was hard. But once I made the decision it was easier. I'm happy."

Lambert paused. "I discovered that anything worthwhile carries a commitment. That's the way life is."

Crow sensed something here. He spoke slowly. "I get the feeling that you're trying to say something profound to me, Lambert. If you are, you can shove it. I don't have any commitments and I don't want any. And I'm happy too."

Lambert spread his hands again. "That's fine then."

Crow's anger was gone again as quickly as it had come. He set the half-filled cup carefully on the table. "Anyway, thanks for the coffee. I have to go now."

"Good luck," Lambert said. "I hope you find her. She's very important to you, isn't she?"

"I just need to find her."

Crow took the dinghy back, made sure to tie it up good and walked to the bus stop.

The fog was thick as ever as he sat by the dirty window. It splintered the headlights on the Coast Highway, shut the riders inside their small cocoon of light.

Crow tried to make his mind work. She wouldn't go back to her mother. Lo Down would still be there, waiting with open arms. She wouldn't go back to Marty. She'd never try that. She would stay away from the police. One of those Runaway Help places? There weren't any in Santa Lucia, but she might try to find one in L.A. He should check that tomorrow. What else was there?

Suddenly the gray, moving swell of the sea flashed into his mind. Crow sat straight and said "No!" so loudly that he wakened the man across the aisle and set two Mexican girls by the door into a fit of giggling. He slumped back. No. She'd never do that again.

But he couldn't get the ocean out of his mind. The emptiness. The black kelp floating . . .

16

Crow wakened early to first light in the sky outside Sasha's window. Immediately he remembered that Valentine was gone, and he wriggled out of the sleeping bag.

The fog had disappeared. Gulls huddled on the beach below.

The pier lay shadowed and empty.

Crow remembered he wasn't going to the shop this morning. There was that dumb photography session with Joe Hollister on the beach at nine. Just what he didn't want, this morning of all mornings.

There was a small sound from the kitchen. Crow spun around. It couldn't be . . . Valentine couldn't have come back. . . . His heart was suddenly soaring, and he ran silently across the softness of Sasha's Indian rug.

The kitchen was empty. No one. His eyes moved across the table—the red paper mats askew, one candle leaning drunkenly to the side, the green fern, the driftwood tree. The pink cake box was moving!

"Get out of there!" Crow yelled.

He crossed the kitchen in three strides, his hands reaching for the box. Too late. Two flat, gray bodies jumped from under the loose lid, raced across the counter and through the gap under the cupboards before he could reach them. He almost got a grip on a long, hairless rat's tail, but it slithered through the gap and away.

Crow looked into the box. One side of the chocolate cake had been eaten. Crumbs lay inches deep on the bottom cardboard, and a small trail of them ran along the counter top where they'd fallen from paws and whiskers during the getaway.

Crow threw the box into the garbage and walked slowly back into the bedroom. He crawled into the sleeping bag and pulled it up and over his head. Go away world. Go away everything. But his thoughts stayed.

In a few minutes he got up again, ate some cereal and went for his shower.

By eight o'clock he was ready, though it was still too early for the beach session. He would read Mrs. Simmons' letter. There was no point in putting it off anymore. Things couldn't get worse.

The envelope held only a drawing. Crow studied it. A small, small figure stood in the middle of a green splash of color. A field, probably. The figure wore what Crow decided was a football uniform and helmet. The shirt had a minuscule M on the front. The arms were stretched out to catch a ball, which floated high in the corner. The only remarkable thing about the drawing was that the figure had just one eye, placed squarely in the middle of the forehead. Underneath, Danny had printed, in letters so small that they were practically not there, the word ME.

Crow turned the drawing sideways to read what Mrs. Simmons had added. "Danny is playing for a Pop Warner football team. It is called the Mighty Mites. He asked me to send you this picture of him in his new uniform. Hope you are well. Love, Aunt L."

Crow wondered if Mrs. Simmons had shown the drawing to Dr. Bustamente and what he'd said. She'd be worried sick if that one-eyed stuff was starting again. She'd wonder what she was doing wrong or what she wasn't doing that she should do.

Well, at least by now she'd know *he* was well. She'd have his letter. He owed her a small accounting of himself, but he didn't owe her anything else. Her or Danny. Crow took a shaky breath. Were those outstretched arms a cry for help? And what about Mrs. Simmons sending the drawing? Was that a cry for help too?

Crow took his wallet from his pocket and slid out the piece of paper he always carried. It was creased and dirty, cracked down the middle. It was another of Danny's drawings. After a night of bad dreams, when Crow had taken Danny and comforted him, he'd come home from school to find a drawing of a giant *Tyrannosaurus rex*, all colored in Crayola, on his bed. It must have taken Danny hours to do it. Underneath it said "TYRANNOSAURUS, KING OF THE BEESTS," and below that the words "I love you, Crow."

The words were smudged away now, but the black marks showed where they'd been. Crow didn't know why he carried the dumb drawing every place he went, but he did. He folded it now and put it back in his wallet. Little Danny. But he still had Mrs. Simmons, didn't he? He didn't need Crow.

Crow sat on the love seat and put his head in his hands. Something heavy as stone had settled in his chest.

There was no way now that he could stay any longer in the apartment. He clicked the door open and went downstairs. The horses waited for him, but he didn't want to talk to them today or go silent riding. For the first time since he'd been here, the big carousel building seemed empty and lonely. He unlocked the outside door and stepped into the morning.

It wasn't nine yet, but he saw that Jim Hollister's Winnebago, the one that was to be their changing room, was already nosing from the Coast Highway onto the pier.

Sam had finished unloading the fish from his old truck and was hosing off the flatbed, shining scales running silver in the stream of water, drying and glittering as they fell. He turned off the hose and came to stand next to Crow, watching the Winnebago limp slowly over the loose pier planks.

"We've got company," he said. "Must have got special permission to come on the pier."

"Yeah," Crow said. "It's a crew making an ad for a magazine. I'm going to be in it."

Sam grinned. "No kidding." He slapped Crow on the back with a wet, fishy hand. "Gonna be a star, huh?"

"I doubt it," Crow said.

The Winnebago stopped and he saw Kim's little, silver Honda nosing onto the pier too.

Crow walked across to the Winnebago. A fancy-looking guy was sitting next to Joe in the passenger seat.

"Great morning, isn't it? Super!" Joe said. "Crow, I want you to meet Cassius, my photographer."

Crow shook the hand Cassius stretched through the open window. He wished he didn't feel so flat and bummed out.

"You've probably seen a lot of Cassius' stuff," Joe said as Cassius stepped out and looked around. "Photography by Cassius?" He lowered his voice. "Confidentially, he's the best there is."

"I've probably seen it," Crow said. "This is my friend Sam, of Sam's Seafood."

Sam flashed his gold teeth. "Pleased to meet you. And, confidentially, I'm the best there is too."

Joe and Cassius both shook Sam's hand. Crow saw Cassius wipe his off on the side of his pale-blue pants.

Kim got out of her Honda and the introductions began all over again.

Cassius eyed her with a professional eye. "You're going to photograph real good, baby," he told her and added, "You too," to Crow.

Joe slid across the back doors of the Winnebago. "All the stuff is laid out back there. Two dressing rooms." He pulled across the Hawaiian print curtain that divided the back of the motor home and grinned his boyish grin. "Now no peeking while she's changing, Crow."

110

Kim giggled. "How about me? I might do a little peeking myself."

As soon as the doors slid shut, Crow shucked his clothes and pulled on the blue shorts with the Wipeout trademark Joe had put on top of the small pile. What did he care, really, about Wipeout or *Surf's Up* magazine? There were too many important things right now that he needed to think about.

The curtain sizzled across.

"How do I look?" Kim stood in the space, smiling at Crow.

She *had* to know how she looked! "Really good," Crow said.

Kim laughed. "Boy, you sure go overboard with the compliments."

Her skin was Hawaiian skin, creamy tan, smooth as satin. And there was lots of it showing. The bikini had two small scraps of scarlet on top and two, just as small, on the bottom. As Kim turned, Crow saw that on the side view she looked as if she wore nothing, poised to dive into some warm, tropical pool, her hair the only color against the warm richness of skin.

Kim's eyes laughed at him. "Well, you look really, really good too, friend Crow."

"Gee thanks!" He pulled open the Winnebago door.

The morning air was chilly and blew Kim's hair out like a pony's mane.

"You're fantastic, wonderful," Cassius told her. "Wait till you see the shots we'll get."

She shivered. "Cold!"

"Here." Joe gave her a big beach towel to wrap around her. "You'll just have to tough it out, Crow."

They went down the steps by the Chart House and Crow saw that already a crowd had gathered. Beach people had an eye for a happening, whether it was a drowning, or a boat washing ashore, or a whale in the water. Or a commercial.

Somebody yelled, "Hey! Crow ducks!" and Crow turned and saw Ethan from the carousel. "I see you've made the big time, love," Ethan shouted, and Crow waved.

Cassius clapped his hands. "OK. Let's get started. Kim! Crow! Here's what I want."

While he listened to Cassius, Crow let his eyes stray around. There must be a hundred people here now. He tilted his head and stared up at the carousel windows. Only yesterday he'd imagined Valentine watching from there.

"You're going to walk up the beach hand in hand," Cassius said. "Just walk. No big acting job. You're two kids who dig each other and you're walking by the

112

ocean. When you get to that rock, turn and come back. Talk to each other. Crow, bend toward her as if you can't get enough of her in her Wipeout bikini. And baby, you do a listening job. Rapt, that's what I want. And don't worry if your hair blows across your face. We like it that way."

"Didn't I tell you he's the best?" Joe murmured.

Kim unwrapped the towel and gave it to Joe. A howl went up from the audience.

Kim smiled. She took Crow's hand and they walked along the waterline, the gulls rising around them in a white beating of wings.

Behind them was Cassius' voice. "Beautiful, wonderful. Let the sea come over your ankles.

"Now turn, turn. There's a great cloud formation behind you. Turn her to face you, Crow. Bend your head. Lick your lips, honey. Give him that adoring look."

Vaguely Crow could hear the shouts in the background.

"Go for it, man!"

"Grab her while you got the chance!"

He looked down into Kim's perfect face, the parted shining lips, the soft dark eyes. His hands were in the hollow of her back, moving against the smooth tingle of skin. He could smell her perfume

113

and feel the way she fitted against him. He knew that this was the girl he used to dream about, lying in his sleeping bag at the bottom of Sasha's bed. But something had changed. He felt nothing now.

The camera clicked and buzzed.

"OK. Wonderful. You can kiss her now."

The crowd cheered.

Crow bent and touched his lips gently to hers. As he drew back he kept his eyes from her face.

"Boo, boo!" the crowd jeered. Someone in the back yelled, "Come on over here, baby, and I'll show you some real kissing!"

"All right," Cassius said. "Whatever's in your hearts. Now, if you go and get changed, I'll reload."

Kim and Crow walked back across the sand. They weren't holding hands now. A distance had sprung up between them that Crow knew might never close again.

"Kim," he began, but she turned her head away.

"We'll have you in the red shorts next, Crow," Joe said. "And Kim, let's try the yellow bikini." He rubbed his hands together. "Gee whillikers but you kids are great!"

Kim ran ahead of him, black hair swinging, and the crowds lining the steps parted to let her through, ohing and ahing and eating her up with their eyes.

Crow walked slowly behind. Why hadn't he wanted to kiss her, anyway? He would have, before. Before what?

"Crow! Hey, Crow!"

Crow turned and saw Ethan.

"Have you heard the news?" Ethan asked. He walked with Crow toward the Winnebago.

"About what?" Crow asked.

"They've finally got the word to tear the carousel down."

"No!"

"Afraid so, ducks. They're moving the merry-go-round over to a piece of ground they've bought opposite the new Plaza mall."

"No," Crow said again. He looked up at the carousel building, at the arched windows with their flaking red paint, at the dome where the pigeons swarmed. Sasha's place. His place.

Ethan smoothed his bald head as if shining it. "It'll probably be good for business."

"The horses will hate it."

Ethan laughed. "Oh, you and those horses!"

"I thought the historical society was fighting it."

Ethan's flat, nasal voice dipped down at the end of sentences and made everything seem so final. "It all

came down to money in the end, ducks. The historical society lost."

"Yeah. I guess . . ." Crow stopped. Over Ethan's
shoulder he saw something that made his heart
slither in his chest. A girl sat on one of the big rocks
between sea and pier. She had her back to him, but
he knew her. The cap, the hunch of the shoulders.

"Valentine," he yelled. And then he was running.

17

Crow ran fast, but Valentine was running too, clam-
bering over the rocks, one of her pink flowered
beach walkers coming off to bounce to the sand
below.

"Valentine! Wait!"

She'd slowed to scoop up the rubber sandal, and he
reached her and grabbed her arm.

"Let me go!"

He held her by the shoulders and shook her
gently. "Why, Valentine? Why did you go off like
that? You scared me half to death. I've been searching everywhere . . . out at Lambert's boat, the pier,
everywhere. Where were you?"

He thought he could see the blaze of her eyes through the dark of the sunglasses.

"You were searching for me? What a joke! I'd have thought you'd be happy."

Joe's furious voice bellowed across the sand. "Hey, guy! Get a move on. You're messing up the whole session."

Crow looked around, frustrated by the staring faces, the curious eyes. And suddenly he remembered that Valentine shouldn't be out in a mob like this and that he shouldn't be drawing attention to her, running after her, shouting out her name.

"Who is the girl?" Valentine asked. "She's pretty. Do you think she is as pretty as Sasha?"

Exasperated, Crow shook his head. "Are you crazy or something, worrying about that now? You've got to get out of sight. Listen, I have to go. Promise me you won't run away again till I have a chance to talk to you. I didn't mean it about you being a problem. Honest. After you left, I . . ." He didn't know how to go on.

"Crow!" Now it was Cassius calling, and Crow saw Kim, already changed into a yellow bikini, standing behind him.

"Look, Valentine. Come back to the Winnebago with me and I'll give you the key to the door. Go up

117

and wait in the secret room. You'll be safe. You can come down when we're finished and let me in." He'd taken hold of her shoulders again, and he bent toward her. "Please."

She stared up at him.

"Please, Valentine." He let all of the desperation he felt come out in his voice.

Slowly she nodded.

"I'll only be a minute changing," Crow told Cassius as they passed him.

Inside the camper he changed quickly into the red shorts and tank top Joe had left out, found the key and took it out to Valentine.

"Wait till everyone's watching the photography," he whispered. "They won't see you go inside."

Standing on the beach, listening to Cassius' instructions, Crow found himself searching for her as she stood by the railing. Seeing her at a distance, part of a crowd, anonymous behind her glasses, he realized again he would know her anywhere.

He smiled sunnily at Kim. "Ready?"

She turned unfriendly eyes on him.

"Uh-oh," he said. "You're still mad. I forgot."

"I always thought those pink beach walkers were tacky," she said.

Crow shrugged. "Maybe she doesn't care." He

looked up at the railing, but Valentine was gone.

Crow did what Cassius directed, splashing knee deep in the surf, scooping up handfuls of water to throw on Kim, who laughed and scampered at the ocean's edge.

"Wonderful! Beautiful! Marvelous!"

It was all so fake. Did people really go for this kind of stuff? Did it make them rush out and buy Wipeout clothes?

At last Cassius stood straight. "That's it, kiddos. *Finito*. The end. You two were . . ."

And then, suddenly, incredibly, Crow heard the carousel calliope blare through the crowds. Cassius stopped in mid sentence.

OH I WENT DOWN SOUTH
FOR TO SEE MY GIRL
SINGING POLLY WOLLY DOODLE
ALL THE DAY . . .

"What's that?" Joe asked.

Crow swung around to stare up at the carousel building, its big front doors locked and bolted. Other people had already turned to gawk, and some were rushing the steps to the pier.

FARE THEE WELL, FARE THEE WELL . . .

119

Crow was running now, pushing past Joe, taking the steps two at a time. It had to be Valentine. She'd stayed below with the horses and for some reason she'd plugged in the calliope.

AND I'M OFF TO LOUISIANA . . .

The music cut off as quickly as it had begun.

Ethan was in the front of the crowd that stood by the big doors of the carousel. He was waving frantically.

"Crow! There's somebody in there," he said. "And I don't have the keys. How did he get in, anyway?"

"The roof," a guy standing at the back suggested. "He could have climbed the wall."

"It's too high without a ladder," someone else said.

Crow was looking at Ethan, and he recognized the instant Ethan remembered the other door.

He and Ethan ran around the side with the crowds bunching behind them.

Ethan pushed on the door. "Locked too. The key to this thing's been lost for ages. I think it got dumped the last time the place was painted."

Crow nodded.

Ethan stepped back. "Well, the calliope couldn't have turned itself on. Do you think we should . . . ?"

120

There was a heavy thud from inside and then silence. The buzz of talk stopped as abruptly as the music had stopped, cutting off Crow's blood along with it. He knew who was inside. Valentine. And something bad had happened.

18

"Valentine!" Crow screamed. But his voice was drowned in the raised voices around them. He pounded on the side door with his fist.

"Should we break it down?" Ethan yelled.

But Joe was beside them now with a small metal saw. "Here." He gave it to Ethan. "I had this in the tool box of the Winnebago. It'll be easier to saw through that padlock on the front."

The crowd jostled aside, letting them get to the double doors.

"You'll never do it," someone offered. "That lock probably has a steel core."

"No it doesn't, ducks," Ethan muttered. "I ought to know. I bought it." The little saw chewed on the soft metal.

Crow felt like pulling it from Ethan's hands and

doing it himself. Hurry, hurry, he urged silently. Valentine's in there. Hurry, hurry.

There was a tug at his arm. Old Sam put his mouth close to Crow's ear and Crow smelled the fishy smell that hung around Sam. "Should I call the cops, Crow?"

Crow bit his lip. Cops nosing around. Valentine wouldn't want that. And he wouldn't either.

"Hold off till we find out what's happening, Sam," he said. "It could be some kid that got in. There's a good chance we can handle it ourselves."

Sam nodded.

Inside the big, round building now there was only silence. The saw grated and ground, and the backs of Ethan's hands were dusted with metal filings, shiny as Sam's fish scales. Finally Crow heard a quick snap.

"Stand back, everyone," Ethan ordered. He pulled the padlock free of the big hasp and pushed open the doors.

Crow saw the carousel turning silently, the horses going up and down on their curly, golden poles. The electric cord from the calliope curled snakelike across the cement floor, where it had been jerked from the wall socket. The place was empty.

He looked up at the circular balcony above the ticket booth and saw a jagged piece of hanging wood.

"Oh, no," he whispered, and began running. Valentine! She'd gone up on the balcony and she'd walked around to where the floor wasn't safe. She'd fallen through. That was the thud. Valentine. Falling to the concrete floor below.

His legs had no feeling. His heart pounded in his ears. Valentine! As he rounded the ticket booth, he saw what he'd known he'd see. She lay on the floor, facedown, crumpled. For a second he was back to the night when he'd pulled her from the sea, back in the dinghy, looking at her lying on her stomach in the pool of dirty water, not knowing if she was alive or dead. He saw again the long legs in the blue jeans . . . and then he saw the white nylon jacket and the white shoes. This wasn't Valentine. Relief made him dizzy. He saw a shock of thick, blond hair. A guy. Strong-looking even as he lay motionless.

"Marty!" Crow whispered. With the new instinct that he seemed to have developed since Valentine had come into his life, he knew it had to be Marty lying there. But where was Valentine?

Ethan was beside him now, staring down at the body, staring up at the broken floor above. He shook his head. "The poor sod!"

Then Joe was beside them too, and Kim, still in her yellow bikini, her skin grayed out somehow, her eyes big with horror. She covered her mouth with her hand.

The crowd kept at a distance.

Crow spoke through numbed lips. "Is he dead? Should we turn him over?" Part of him didn't want to look. Another part needed to know how bad it was.

Ethan kneeled down. "I don't think we should mess with him."

Someone behind said, "That old guy who was here? The fish man? He's gone to call for an ambulance."

Ethan put his hand on the side of Marty's neck and said, "I can't feel a pulse. But I don't know from nothing. I don't suppose there's a doctor in the house?"

No one spoke.

Crow made himself kneel too. Now he could see Marty's face with the head turned sideways. The eyes were closed. A white bandage across his nose looked fresh and clean, as if it had been stuck on this morning.

"Looks like he had a broken nose. Have you ever seen the bloke before, Crow?" Ethan asked.

Crow shook his head. "Never."

They all waited in silence. Crow wished that somehow he could slip away to go look for Valentine.

124

Where was she? Up above them somewhere? Safe in the secret room? Or had she taken off again, running scared when the doors opened and the crowd pressed in?

And then Sam was back, pushing through to stand beside them. He rubbed his hands nervously up and down the sides of his white apron. "The ambulance is coming," he told Ethan. And as if by magic they heard the faraway sound of a siren and another wailing behind it with a different pitch and intensity.

"Coppers, too," Ethan said.

Crow felt his heart lurch. Of course there'd be cops. The guy might be dead. There'd be questions and searching and eyes that suspected everything. He stepped back, making himself part of the crowd.

The carousel was still turning silently. Maximilian and Daphne and Cleo smiled their painted smiles, dancing to the joy of remembered music.

I wish you a ride on the merry-go-round, Crow thought. He tried to stand still and anonymous in the crowd.

It was the paramedics who arrived first. They checked Marty's pulse. He was still alive. But they didn't move him or turn him over till the police came and tramped all around him. Then they put him on a stretcher and carried him to the ambulance.

"Is the poor bloke going to make it?" Ethan asked the paramedics. "He doesn't look too healthy."

"It's too soon to say. You'll have to check later with the hospital."

The police moved everybody but Ethan outside. Crow stood with the onlookers, trying to hear as Ethan told them about how there'd been first the carousel music, then the thud, and how they'd sawed the lock off to get in. The cops took notes. Then they disappeared up the side stairs with Ethan in the lead.

They'd never find the secret room, Crow told himself. And Valentine was safe inside. He told himself that too. But what if Marty had gotten to her before he fell? What if he'd hurt her, hurt her bad? What if Ethan or one of the cops yelled out, "Get another ambulance here on the double. There's a girl. She's got sort of red hair and the biggest green eyes and terrific legs. Funny-looking shoes. She's been beaten up bad. She's unconscious . . . bleeding . . . broken."

Crow bit at his knuckles.

The cops and Ethan came down and stood talking in front of the cop car. Then the officers drove away.

Ethan came across to Crow. "Well, there's no one else in there. It looks like it was an accident. The bloke was mooching around above and . . . well, you know how the flooring is. A bloody good thing it's all being torn down before someone else gets hurt!"

Crow nodded. "Yeah. It does make you think."

"The cops can't figure how he got in, though. Of course, there is that open window where my pigeons are. Maybe he did climb the wall somehow. They don't know why he turned on the merry-go-round, either. Brady—he's one of the coppers—Brady says the bloke could have been high on PCP or something. They'll find out when they get him to the hospital."

"Are they sure there's nobody else?" Crow asked.

"There's nowhere for anyone to hide up there, except maybe in one of the old broom closets. They checked everywhere. By the way, the guy's name is John Gerald Martin. He lives here, in Santa Lucia. He was carrying a driver's license."

Crow closed his eyes. John Gerald Martin. Marty. The name made him seem like a person suddenly, and Crow didn't like it.

Joe butted through the crowd. "Man, I hate to mention such small stuff at a time like this. But if you'd change back into your own things, Crow, Cassius and I could be on our way." He lowered his voice. "Confidentially, this whole business has upset Cassius a lot. He's very sensitive."

"I'm sure." Crow glanced down at the red shorts and shirt he'd forgotten he was wearing. "I'll change right now," he said.

"And after you do, Crow, can you come back and stick around here for a while?" Ethan asked. "I have to go get a new lock. I can't leave the place lying open."

"OK." Crow's mind was working again, the wheels turning. "Can somebody tell them at the shop what happened and that I won't be in for a while?"

"I will," Kim said.

Crow vaguely remembered that he and Kim hadn't been too friendly today. But that was a long time ago and it didn't matter anymore.

He changed quickly into his own clothes and came back to the carousel.

The mob was breaking up, heading again for the beach. Crow was glad. All he wanted now was the chance to go upstairs and find out, one way or the other.

As soon as Ethan went, Crow closed the doors. Then he walked across and pressed the button that shut off the carousel.

The horses slowed, coming lazily, dreamily to a standstill.

He felt them watching him as he climbed the stairs that led up and up to the secret room.

19

He saw her as soon as he opened the door. She stood in the middle of the secret room, the cap gone now, the sun turning her hair to copper gold. She was like one of the carousel horses, frozen in time.

And then she ran to him, clinging, burying her face against his neck.

"Sh," he whispered. "Don't. It's all right."

She was talking, the words spilling over each other, muffled against his throat.

"He was out there. He came through the door behind me. He pushed me. I crawled onto the carousel with him after me. Somehow I found the starter button. I thought he'd fall, but he didn't. He kept coming. And then I remembered the music, and that you were outside, and for a minute he couldn't find the plug to shut it off. Oh, Crow!" She lifted her face to him. There was dirt smeared across her chin and a cobweb glittered in her hair. He pulled it gently away.

"Is Marty dead?"

"No. He's not dead. He's hurt bad, though. He fell through the boards."

"I know." She shuddered and her head went down again. "I almost fell with him. I ran up the stairs, to get away. But I was afraid to come into the secret room because he would have seen me, and then the secret place would be lost to you forever. So I ran, and he caught me. . . ."

She was shaking again and he soothed her with his hands. "Sh, sh."

"He had just grabbed my arm. I heard the wood splinter and I jumped back." She hiccuped, that same, funny, little-kid sound that he remembered. "He didn't even scream as he fell. He just . . . dropped."

Crow put his lips against her hair. It smelled salty, like the ocean. It smelled musty, like the old building around them. She was part of it all, as he was.

"And then I heard the pounding and I knew you had come. I ran in here."

"That was right," Crow murmured. "That was OK."

Valentine moved a little away from him. "Is Marty going to die? I hate him and I'm scared of him. But I don't think I want him to die."

"I can't tell you that, sweetheart." He heard the word as soon as he said it. "Sweetheart." Where had *that* come from? Such a weird, old-fashioned word. He didn't know he even knew it. He rushed on to cover it up.

"Look. I don't want to leave you like this, but Ethan will be back any minute with a new lock and he'll wonder where I disappeared to. Will you stay here? Make some tea. I won't be long. I promise. Do you still have the key?"

She took it with trembling hands from her pocket and gave it to him.

"I'll be back." He couldn't believe how hard it was to leave her. What had happened to the Crow who flew alone?

20

Crow pulled on the new lock and chain that Ethan had brought. "All secure," he said. "Let's go."

They walked together to the end of the pier.

"Cheerio," Ethan said.

"See you." Crow stood by the traffic light as though waiting to cross, then doubled back.

The kettle boiled on the kitchen stove. Crow saw that Valentine had washed the dirt from her hands and face and combed her hair. She was pale, and somehow like a little girl who could use her mother. But she didn't have an available mother any more than he did. He wanted to put his arms around her again, but there was an awkwardness. The emergency was over. She might not want him to hold her now. And he didn't think he could stand it if she pushed him away.

"I don't suppose you heard anything more about Marty?" She stood at the table with her back to him, pouring the boiling water into two blue mugs.

"I'll phone the hospital in a little while," Crow said. "They probably wouldn't know anything yet."

Her back was stiff and tense, and she stood for a long time with the kettle in her hand. Crow searched for something neutral to say.

"Hey! You cleaned up the kitchen. I left a mess." Shoot! That wasn't neutral. What a dummy he was!

Valentine put the kettle on the stove. "I cleaned it this morning. Before I went out."

Crow stared at her. "What do you mean, before you went out?"

She dabbled her teabag in the mug. "I was in the

carousel building all night. I slept in Ethan's beanbag chair."

Crow put his hands on the table and leaned across it. "You were here? While I was searching the . . ." He stopped. "I checked this whole place."

"I heard you." Her voice was so casual he wanted to shake her.

"I hid on the roof with the pigeons. When you left I came back inside and waited for morning. And I thought a lot. About what I should do. About where I could go where someone would want me."

Crow slumped. Now he needed to hold her again. This girl made him do so many turnarounds it was driving him crazy.

"And when you left again this morning, I went into the apartment and got the cap and glasses." She lifted her head. "Not that my disguise did any good in the end. It didn't fool Marty."

Crow couldn't get over it. He'd seen her in the cap and glasses and he hadn't even remembered she'd run out last night without them. Some detective he'd make.

"Truly, Crow, I never expected you'd bother to search. I still don't know why you did."

It was Crow's turn to concentrate on his teabag. He moved it around, making the water darker, just the way he didn't like it. She didn't know why? What if he told her? What if he said, "You're important to me, that's why?" "Important how?" she'd ask. "I don't know," he'd say. "I only know you are." Instead he said, "No one's going to be in this secret place much longer. The building's definitely coming down."

Her eyes were wide. "No! You thought that might happen, didn't you? What about the horses?"

"They'll move them from here to the mall."

"The horses will hate it," Valentine said.

They were the exact words he'd used. How strange.

"I know. But there'll still be kids to ride them and they'll be outside, smelling the wind and the sea. They'll have each other."

Valentine leaned back in her chair. "Does Sasha know?"

"No. Maybe. I'm not sure."

"Aren't you going to tell her?"

"I have no way to . . . to get in touch with her."

Valentine straightened a frond on the green fern. "Crow? Why don't you tell me about Sasha?"

"You already know, don't you?" Crow asked.

"I began to guess the day I went to the library."

Crow sat for a few seconds and then pushed back

his chair and stood. He went to Sasha's bedroom and took the diary from the bottom drawer of the big wardrobe where he'd first found it. The half page of newspaper was folded inside it. He took it out and opened it so only the top part showed. Two photographs smiled from the printed page.

"It's Sasha," Valentine said. "The same picture that's in the bedroom." Her finger moved to the other picture. It showed an old lady in a droopy hat. The eyes were wise as the eyes of an old turtle. They smiled at the camera, knowing everything, forgiving everything. "That's Sasha too," Valentine said. "It's the same smile."

Crow reached forward and unfolded the other half of the clipping. The headline said:

ACTRESS SASHA SEVILLE DIES IN NICE, FRANCE

Actress Sasha Seville, who appeared in thirty-two films during the silent era and made herself a minor legend, has died at the age of eighty-eight.

Miss Seville appeared in her first talkie in 1938 with Randolph Scott. She was in several films with the then child star Milton Berle.

Columnist Earl Wilson dubbed her The Lady of Mystery because she occasionally dropped out of sight, only to mysteriously reappear, lovelier than ever.

"In my secret place I renew my spiritual strength," she said. Where was that secret place? No one knows.

Miss Seville's last film appearance at the age of sixty-four was in the Paramount picture *The Truth About Ellie.*

Funeral arrangements are incomplete.

Valentine turned the paper over, scanning the back. "Oh, Crow. How awful! When was this?"

"It was in July, after I found the secret room. But before I moved in. I'd seen her picture in the bedroom. Seen it? I knew it by heart. One day, when I was going home to the dump I rented with another guy, I saw her picture staring up at me from the front of the L.A. *Times.*" He rubbed his hand across his face. "Maybe she meant to come back here in the end. Maybe she was too ill or too old. I tried to find out about those funeral arrangements, but of course no one knew. I would have liked to go. It was probably in Nice anyway." He ran out of words and stood, looking down at the two pictures, the usual lump coming in his throat.

"There was something about Sasha. I knew she'd understand if I wanted to move in here. I needed a place too. I never have had my own place. There was the orphanage. Then the foster homes, one after the other."

He turned the diary in his hands. "I found this. I didn't read past page one. You'll see why."

He gave the square leather book to Valentine and watched her open it to the first page.

"Above these shining horses I will find my peace," Valentine read, her voice tender as the words themselves. "This will be my secret place, and to this secret book I will trust my thoughts."

She folded the clipping and slipped it between the pages of the diary. Then she closed the book gently and placed it in Crow's hands.

"You were a good caretaker, Crow. You kept guard over her secret place and her secret thoughts. You did just one thing wrong. You fell in love with her."

"I know."

21

Crow had to go back to work in the afternoon. Valentine walked beside him along the pier. "I never did tell you about Marty," Valentine said. "Not really." She looked across the ocean, where giant sunstruck waves surged in to shore.

"Marty goes on little recruiting trips. He did, I

mean. Small towns, unhappy girls, smooth talk. I thought he cared about me. He was in Fayette . . ." She looked at Crow briefly. "Fayette, Indiana. That's where I live. Lived. He was there for just four days. And in those four days he told me all I was missing. All the love. All the opportunities. I didn't care about the opportunities. It was the love I wanted. He was gentle and sweet. I told him about Lo Down and how my mother had turned against me. Marty didn't try to touch me, though. But I wanted him to."

She'd wanted him to! Crow bent down and pretended to tie his shoe lace. "Wait up a sec, Valentine." She'd wanted him to!

"Marty said that he loved me too much, that if he started touching me he'd never stop." She gave a little laugh that could just as easily have been a sob. "Anyway . . . after he left, he wrote about how much he missed me. He sent money for a bus ticket and he sent the necklace. He said he'd seen it, and he wanted me to have it, to remember him." Again that half laugh, half sob. "Lo Down was getting worse. He came in my room one night when Mom was out. He sat on my bed and his hand came creeping under the covers. I locked myself in the bathroom and stayed there till Mom came home. There was no use trying to tell her again." Valentine sighed. "Maybe she did

138

believe me, but to admit it would have meant leaving him. Easier to let me go, I guess."

She was walking so quickly that Crow had to lengthen his stride to keep up.

"So I went. I went to Marty. He was dear and loving, at first. He didn't push me. I needed time, he said. When he began saying weird things, I didn't get it. About how he had these wonderful friends and how they shared everything. I didn't get it at all. Then, one day, a girl came when Marty was out. She was about my age. She said her name was Rose. Right off she asked me if I was one of Marty's 'girls.' I was so dumb, I thought she meant one of his girlfriends and I was kind of jealous. Then Marty came home unexpectedly. He was furious. He hit Rose, real hard. He said she knew better than to come to his apartment. All his girls knew that. His place was off limits after initiation. That's what he said. After initiation."

Crow reached out and touched her hand, but she pulled it angrily away. He knew suddenly that she'd be angry for a long, long time whenever she thought of Marty.

"After Rose left, Marty tried to put his arms around me, all the time talking this sweet, stupid talk, telling me I was different, saying I didn't understand. I understood all right. He had this bronze statue on his

139

coffee table. Pan, playing his little pipes. I hit him with it." Crow saw her hand come up, remembering. "I meant to hit him on the back, but he turned and . . . and then I ran. Oh, Crow. I was so sick and ashamed. It was pretty soon after that that you dragged me out of the ocean." This time it was a laugh all right, filled with bitterness. "Imagine! Trying to kill myself over a rat like Marty! He was so mad at me, Crow, and there was blood everywhere. On his white couch. On his white rug. Pouring out of his nose. And he was choking and screaming about how I'd cost him bucks already. How nobody did this to him and got away with it." She shaded her eyes as if they hurt. "I suppose I should let go of the hate now. I mean, he's . . ."

Crow wished he could help, somehow. He glanced sideways at her. Ragamuffin girl in her dirty clothes. Not beautiful. Not even pretty. His heart was melting.

"I made a phone call this morning," she said. "It came out of all that thinking last night."

He tried to keep his voice even. "Did you call your mother?"

Valentine shook her head. "No. I called Aunt Midge. You know, my mom's friend in Utah."

"The one who has twelve dogs?"

"She has thirteen now. She took in one that has only three legs. She's taking me too."

It wasn't easy to stay cool when his heart was doing all these strange things. Crow felt as if he had a few broken circuits.

"That's nice," he said, as if the fact that she was leaving was totally normal. Which it was. "You ought to be safe with her. Anybody who'd take in thirteen dogs, and one of them with only three legs, has to be OK."

"Anyway, I guess I'll get to start another garden. Aunt Midge says there's an overgrown part of the yard. It's fenced off from the dogs and I can have it, if I like. I had cucumbers this year, and summer squash. . . ." She stopped. "I hope Mom . . ." She stopped again.

"A garden's good," Crow said. He had a sudden picture of her, on her knees, digging in Aunt Midge's yard. He saw the dogs, barking joyously at the fence, trying to get to her. The winter was over and the Utah sky was blue. He saw Valentine's face, and she was happy. He jammed his hands into the pockets of his corduroys. "When do you go?"

Valentine stooped to pick up a shell no bigger than her fingernail. "Tomorrow. She's wiring me money to the post office in Santa Lucia. It's a big deal be-

141

cause I have no ID, but she was going to call the postmaster and give him a description of me."

"That Bloomingdale's sweat shirt should be as good as a full set of fingerprints," Crow said lightly.

Valentine held up the shell to the light. "I told Aunt Midge about Lo Down. She says there's no way I should go back there till Mom comes to her senses. I wouldn't, anyway. She says I can finish high school, and she and I'll figure something out."

Crow faked interest in a guy drawing a picture of the pier with Magic Marker pens.

"You're going tomorrow, huh?" He decided maybe he should be an actor. He was coming on friendly, but not too friendly. Semi-interested. "Well, you're welcome to spend one last night in the carousel. And I tell you what. Tonight I'll take you out for a bust-up dinner. We'll go the Chart House. It'll make up for the beef stuff."

"Beef bourguignon." She smiled. "A farewell feast. And soon you'll be leaving too, leaving the carousel, leaving Sasha. You'll be the old crow, flying off to newer pastures or wherever it is old crows fly."

"Taller trees, warmer nests," Crow said, and he smiled too. If she could smile about it, well so could he.

22

It was after two before Crow got in to work. He'd left Valentine sitting on the beach, down where they'd run among the sand castles with the little yellow dog, where she'd seen her house get washed away. It all seemed so long ago.

"I had to send Kim home," Rob said. "She was totally flipped. What with the photography stuff and then seeing that guy who fell in the carousel."

"Yeah. It was bad, all right." Crow was glad Kim wasn't here. He wished *he* wasn't.

He thought about Valentine waiting for him. It excited him. But there was another feeling too, nervousness. Anyway, she was going. That was good. It was safer. Tonight they'd have the farewell dinner and they'd stay together one last time in the carousel. He'd try to keep his mind from going any farther than that.

But they didn't go out for a farewell dinner after all.

"Nothing to wear," Valentine said. "I know that's what girls are supposed to say. But this time it's true."

Crow shook his head. "Why didn't I think of that? I could have picked up a new sweat shirt for you at the shop. It would have been nice for you to have something clean when you leave."

"There you go again, starting with that 'when I leave' bit." You can't wait, can you?"

"That's not what I meant. Look, I don't even want . . ." Crow stopped. He didn't know what he wanted.

Valentine took a deep breath. "This sweat shirt's all right. But not for dinner in the Chart House."

"OK. OK. I understand." Crow went out again and bought chilled crab legs from Sam's, and a loaf of crusty bread and a bottle of sparkling golden cider. He bought an avocado and tomatoes, bursting with sweetness. And he thought about it and finally bought a chocolate cake too, in a pink box—not quite the same as the one she'd had for him, but close.

When he got back, the kitchen table was set, the candles lit, the fern in the center spreading itself in spiky, green fronds. She'd cut the place mats heart shaped this time, and when Crow touched one she said, "It's not February, I know. But I thought we might pretend it's Valentine's Day."

"The color's right." Crow saw that she'd turned her sweat shirt right side out so that the big BLOOM-

INGDALE'S letters marched across the front the way they'd done on the first night. He couldn't help noticing the bumps again, the ones that had first clued him in that she was a girl. He hadn't been able to forget that she was a girl since. He looked quickly away. Someday he'd be in a city where they had a Bloomingdale's, and he'd stop and examine the sign above the door, looking for those mysterious bumps. He'd know that this sign had something missing. It just didn't have the pizzazz of one he'd seen somewhere before.

He gave her the paper sack he was carrying. "Crab for dinner. And I bought vegetables and stuff. And a cake." He watched her lift the lid to peer inside the pink box, watched her remember.

"We need more water," he said, and before she could speak he went to get it.

The pigeons flapped excitedly when they heard his step. "Cool it," he said. "It's only Crow." He stuck a finger through the mesh wire. "Poor things! I guess Ethan's going to have to find another home for you, too. All us birds are going to need new nests."

When he came back, Valentine had everything ready. The crab was piled high on a platter. The avocadoes were peeled and ringed with the scarlet tomatoes.

145

"I wonder if avocadoes grow in Utah," Valentine said. "They're such a pretty green." She touched the table. "It's a perfect color combination."

"I try to think of everything," Crow told her.

He hadn't thought of how they were going to crack the crab legs, though, and he had to go down to the tool box in the carousel and bring up pliers.

They sat opposite one another and passed the pliers back and forth, picking the meat from the coral shells.

"Pliers have a lot of class," Valentine said.

Crow nodded. "I'll never use anything else on crabs again."

Afterward he made coffee and they cut the cake, sitting in the warmth of the flickering candles, not talking much, letting the night come down slowly around them. When the candles were only pools of wax, they left the kitchen and went into Sasha's living room. Crow turned the velvet love seat so it faced the window and the sky, where stars lay scattered like daisies. Below them, the yellow pier lamp hung bright as a Chinese lantern.

"It's sad to think of the wreckers coming and turning all this into rubble," Valentine said. "Will you try to save some of Sasha's things, Crow?"

Crow was aware of her shoulder touching his, of the long warmth of her beside him. He sat rigid, cradling his coffee cup.

"I'd almost decided to keep her diary and the picture in the bedroom," he said. "But I don't think she'd want that. This was her secret place. It's better if it disappears and stays a secret forever."

Valentine had turned her head. He felt the whisper of her breath against his cheek. Suppose he turned too? They'd be so close, their lips almost touching. Instead he leaned forward and set his coffee cup on the floor, and dangled his hands between his knees.

Over in the Chart House the night's dancing had started. The music drifted up to them, the sad, sweet moan of a trumpet, the lonely wail of a trombone. It was Mrs. Simmons' kind of music, filled with good-byes and lost loves. It tugged at his heart. What was wrong with him? He felt like bawling. Valentine was going tomorrow. But so what? This was just another episode in the life of the Crow who flew alone . . . who flew alone because that was the way he wanted it.

Snatches of words drifted up to them.

Once, in a time that's past
I thought love would last. . . .

Dumb to think that, Crow thought. Dumb to love anyone.

Valentine was standing up, and somehow he was too and they were moving together to the music. There was enough space between them for two other persons to dance and Crow thought maybe two did. Marty. And Sasha.

I'm afraid to care
Life can be unfair,
Love is all too rare.

The guy sang as if he were ready to bawl himself. Crow swallowed to ease the ache in his throat.

When the music stopped they did too, facing one another, his hands at her waist and hers on his shoulders. The space was still there, the ghosts watchful between them.

"I'm still very scared," Valentine said. "I hope I won't always be scared."

Crow took a deep breath. "I think you'll get over it. Later. When you meet someone you love and feel safe with."

He felt himself shaking. He was looking into her eyes and he knew he didn't want her to meet someone and fall in love.

148

"You know what?" he said slowly. "I'm scared too. I think I'm scared of you."

Valentine's smile trembled. "I've known that all along. But I can't figure out why."

Crow pulled her closer. When he spoke it wasn't only to her—it was to himself.

"I'm scared because you're starting to be . . . important to me. And I don't want anyone to be important in my life, because just when you begin to care and feel safe, the person sends you away. Everyone I've ever cared about has sent me away, beginning, I guess, with my mother. Only Mrs. Simmons and Danny didn't. Instead, I went, before it could happen with them."

"Maybe it wouldn't have," Valentine said.

Crow swallowed. "And Sasha, of course. It was OK to love Sasha. She was safe."

Valentine was stroking his hair, soothing him the way he soothed Danny after a bad dream.

She pulled back so she could see his face. "Isn't it strange, Crow, that we're two of a kind? We're just turned around, that's all. I ran away to find love. You ran away from love. Crazy!"

They stood in silence, the lamplight washing around them, the music throbbing from the pier, the old building warming and comforting them.

"Like two halves of a puzzle," Crow said. "Do you think we should put the puzzle together?"

"Now?" Valentine asked.

Crow raised his eyebrows. "It seems like the perfect place and the perfect time to me." The words were cool and filled with self-confidence, but he wasn't. What if she said, "Bug off!" Or worse?

Her lips parted.

Crow leaned forward and kissed her. He laid his hands tenderly on either side of her face.

"Darling Valentine," he whispered. "If I asked you, would you stay?"

"Darling Crow," Valentine said. "Thank you, oh, thank you for asking. But I couldn't. I have things to finish and so do you." She turned from him suddenly and lifted her hair. "Can you take this off for me?" Her fingers touched the clasp of Marty's necklace. "I've decided that the trick isn't to keep remembering how stupid you've been. The trick is to forget."

Crow undid the necklace and held it in the palm of his hand. "What shall I do with it?"

"Leave it here. Let it go with everything else." She smiled up at him. "You know, you have the most gorgeous nose. And by the way, what's your name?"

"Charles Robert O'Neill. What's yours?"

"Valentine Love. Didn't I tell you my father was a romantic?"

Later, they lay side by side on the comforter, holding hands under the sleeping bag. A space was still between them, but no ghosts lay there. It was a space of their own making and Crow knew that one day it would be gone.

Her voice came out of the shadows. "Where will you go when you leave here, Crow?"

"I'm not sure. Maybe back to Illinois. To Mrs. Simmons and Danny. I think they need me." It was another commitment, and he'd need a little more time to get ready for it. But he thought he could. "I have some money saved. I'd like to take woodworking classes. But I'll stay here with the horses till the end. I couldn't leave them."

"Perhaps you'll make your own carousel someday," Valentine said softly. "With wonderful, shining horses."

Crow smiled in the dark. "Maybe I will."

"Will you write to me?" Valentine asked.

"What do you think?"

"Crow? Is it far from Illinois to Utah?"

Crow smiled and squeezed her hand. "It can't be that far," he said. "Not as the Crow flies."

About the Author

EVE BUNTING is the winner of the 1976 Golden Kite Award and the recipient of the 1977 Best Work of Fiction Award of the Southern California Council on Literature for Children and Young People. She has written over one hundred books for children, including three other Page-Turners published by Lippincott, THE CLOVERDALE SWITCH, THE WAITING GAME and THE GHOSTS OF DEPARTURE POINT.

Ms. Bunting was born in Ireland, and since 1958 she has lived with her husband and three children in California, where she works as a teacher and lecturer.